PURE SEX

PURE SEX

LUCINDA BETTS
BONNIE EDWARDS
SASHA WHITE

APHRODISIA

KENSINGTON BOOKS

http://www.kensingtonbooks.com

KENSINGTON BOOKS are published by

Kensington Publishing Corp.
850 Third Avenue
New York, NY 10022

ISBN: 0-7582-1466-9

First Trade Paperback Printing: July 2006
10 9 8 7 6 5 4 3 2 1

Printed in the United States of America

THE BET

LUCINDA BETTS

1

Gritting her teeth, Zoe trailed her colleagues—all men—into the bar for happy-hour drinks. Their laughter filled the place, and jealousy zinged through her. What they'd achieved so effortlessly, she'd never mastered. Oh, she had the Midas touch when it came to investments, but the easy camaraderie, the feeling like she played on their team . . . for her that was nearly impossible to obtain.

"What'll you have?" the bartender asked as she shrugged off her black wool coat.

"Club soda with lime, please," she answered, hoping only the bartender heard. She wanted to look like one of the guys, and the guys drank.

Moments later, a martini appeared. A red explosion swirled in the olive's place.

"What's this?" she asked the bartender.

"An atomic fireball."

"Like the jawbreaker?"

"That's what's at the bottom."

Her mouth watered. "But I didn't order it."

"It's from one of the guys," he answered, nodding at the men from her firm.

"Really? Which one?"

"The leader of the pack over there."

"Oh," she said, looking where the bartender pointed. Phillip Kingdom, dark hair shining, smiled at her. Zoe tried not to appreciate the strong line of his jaw, but ignoring his dimpled grin was harder. She raised the glass to him in a stoic thanks.

"He said the drink's a lot like you," the bartender added, walking away.

That sounded like something Phillip would say.

Even from across the room Phillip admired the curve of her breast in that silk shirt. Hoping the fireball had loosened her up, he waited until she'd emptied the glass before he walked over to her. "Why aren't you dancing, Lauterborn?" he asked, sliding a second martini in front of her.

"I have a better question—why the drinks?"

He laughed. "That's a hell of a 'thank you.' You should have been a lawyer."

"What? And missed a career where I'm the only woman in the entire department?"

"I should have guessed that was the attraction."

"Did you think it was the ethereal call of mutual funds?"

"It was for me." An image of his father and grandfather flashed through his mind. They'd both been wildly successful in banking and investing.

"That explains the wingtips."

"You're going to pick on my shoes?"

"You can take it."

"If I can't, there are a dozen or so other guys willing to try."

"I don't want to make all of you cry."

"Just me? At least you've noticed me."

Zoe laughed, tilting her face toward the ceiling. Phillip imagined running his lips from her collarbone to her ear. Yum.

"Come dance with me."

"Why?"

"Let's see . . . You're the most beautiful woman in the joint. Probably the smartest person, too . . ."

She rolled her eyes at his blatant flattery, even while grinning.

"Wondering why you should dance with me?"

"Exactly."

"Because you've knocked back a martini and started on a second, sitting here alone. Drinking by yourself isn't a good sign."

Zoe waved at the surrounding throng. "I'm hardly alone. Besides, you're here."

"Do you use some hex to keep the wolves at bay, or is it your sheer force of will?"

"Obviously neither. It hasn't kept you away." Phillip laughed again at her tenacity. In months of these conversations, he'd never actually won a sparring match. His earnings rarely beat hers either. Damn it.

"I think you just called me a wolf."

"But I didn't call you big or bad." The way her voice slid over the words let him know exactly what she was thinking. The edgy excitement he always felt while talking with her flooded through him.

"I could be very bad. If you don't watch it, you'll never know."

"Oh, really."

"I could take off those glasses, pull your hair out of that bun. You and me and that Cuban beat . . ."

For a moment she didn't react. His heart raced. Would she finally slap him?

Worse. Her spine stiffened, and the sparkle evaporated. "Not a chance," she said.

Phillip stifled his irritation, but he'd had enough. He'd tried all the customary ways of asking her out, getting her attention. None had worked. She flirted sometimes, but she never went out with him. She never went out with any of the guys. He needed to try something untraditional, something . . . different, maybe dangerous. But what?

"So," he said after the pause, "I bet you want that promotion as badly as I do."

"Yeah, I want it."

Phillip ignored the opportunity for a suggestive remark and said, "One of us is going to get it."

Zoe laughed, but it wasn't the warm sound of minutes ago. "When was the last time your earnings were higher than mine?"

She was right, but winning was in his blood.

"A while," he was forced to agree.

"And when was the last time the firm gave a promotion to anyone besides the highest earner?"

Phillip knew she had him. She was like that. "You'll look great in that black leather chair." Not that she'd be sitting there any time soon.

She grinned at his comment. "I'd love that corner office."

No one could say Zoe Lauterborn didn't deserve the promotion, but that didn't mean he wouldn't try his damndest to get it. And Phillip knew a few facts about this firm that hardworking Miss Lauterborn couldn't even imagine.

This firm had never promoted a woman—not until they absolutely had to.

"Last chance to dance," he offered, standing and extending his hand toward her. She shook her head, as he knew she would, but the hot secretary from the twelfth floor saved him when she slid her hand suggestively over his shoulder and said, "I'll dance, Phillip."

"Later, Lauterborn," he said as he led the other woman to the dance floor. Was that irritation he saw in her gaze? Maybe he was making some headway. Half a plan was formulating in the back of his mind. He'd have her yet.

Twenty minutes later Zoe Lauterborn realized her mistake—at least one of them. She should have stuck with club soda. The vodka made her lips numb, and watching him dance left her . . . restless. That had to be the booze. He matched his partner's moves beat for beat. Zoe couldn't look away. Her imagination covered his naked chest in war paint and put him around a bonfire. She'd paint him herself, with her fingertips.

She tore her gaze away from him, annoyed with herself. Phillip Kingdom was a colleague, a competitor. Completely off limits.

But Zoe's resolution lasted only seconds. She wished he'd come back so she could tease him some more. She wished she could slide her hand over his shoulder and say, "I'll dance with you, Phillip," in a sultry voice.

For a moment Zoe wondered if the cost of being the best investment banker on Wall Street was too high. She'd been running with the wolves too long. When was the last time she'd danced to tantalize her partner or slid into silk panties in anticipation of having them ripped off? A craving to flash her thigh or tattoo unicorns on her derriere overwhelmed her. Zoe wanted to do something uncharacteristic, something wild. And she wanted to do it now.

She was losing her mind. Damn Phillip Kingdom for sending her those drinks, and damn her pathetic self for drinking them.

* * *

As Zoe was sitting alone, her colleagues settled around her, and Zoe stifled a groan. She needed to get away from Phillip before she did something she regretted—like drink a third martini.

Phillip didn't make it easier. He pressed his leg against hers under the table, and she knew it wasn't because of the crowd's crush. Feeling reckless, bulletproof, Zoe didn't move away. The drinks coursing through her magnified the texture of his gabardine wool pants against her thigh. She shifted, just a bit, closer.

Zoe watched Phillip laugh with the guy next to him. His easy camaraderie was damn sexy. But if—no, when—she got the promotion, these guys would work for her. She needed their respect and support, which meant she could be their buddy but not their girlfriend. Why she allowed herself to flirt with Phillip every Friday night defied rational explanation.

"So, who's going to be the new head?" one of them asked her from across the table.

I am. "Whoever sold the most in the last six months, probably," she answered, relieved to hear her voice clear, if a little too loud.

She drank again, savoring her private happiness. Her latest client, a stoic New Englander with old money, had canceled today's appointment—some sort of family emergency—but at 11:30 next Monday, he was scheduled to sign on the dotted line. Her dotted line. Once he did, she'd break all company records. Zoe knew she was hot, unstoppable. She could practically taste her promotion.

"That going to be you, Kingdom?" asked McMurtry.

What? Zoe tried to school her shock. How could they even think it might be him? He consistently ran second to her.

Haas took it upon himself to answer. "Of course it'll be

Kingdom. He has a direct line to the Fed Chairman. Like the Batphone, only better."

Zoe knew she should laugh—the joke was funny—but the comment pissed her off. All these Friday-night happy hours, and they still never took her seriously. God, what did she have to do for them to respect her talent?

"If I have the Batphone, Lauterborn has a psychic hotline," Phillip said. Even through the martinis Zoe started. Maybe she'd thank him by . . . *no, no, no.* Sleeping with a colleague would not earn their esteem. Sheet-burning sex with Phillip Kingdom was not in the plan. Any plan.

Haas snorted sarcastically. "Right. Lauterborn."

"Better watch out, Haas. She could be your next boss," said Phillip.

"If she ever lightened up, maybe," said McMurtry.

Frustrated and angry, the words flew out. "I manage better than any of you and that's a fact. You can look at the online rooster-roster any time you're curious."

"I bet you don't get the position, Lauterborn. You won't sell more than Kingdom." The certain glint in his eye hardened something inside of her.

"Really? Want to stake your bonus?" she asked, riding the vodka wave of confidence.

"Uh . . ." Clearly, no one wanted to risk that much money. Haas wasn't drunk enough. Neither was McMurtry.

"You're all talk. You don't have the balls." She stood wobbly on her high heels and headed out the door with what she hoped was dignity.

Even as Phillip admired the way her black skirt hugged her hips, the idea gelled. The plan was devious and probably unethical. If he paused to think about it even for a moment, he'd likely change his mind.

So he didn't stop—he ran with it. The set-up was perfect, irresistible. And most ironically, Zoe had laid the groundwork for it herself—she'd done so perfectly.

"Hey Haas, toss that napkin this way, will you?" commanded Phillip as he reached for his pen.

He'd get Zoe Lauterborn's attention, at least once, come hell or high water.

2

The Manhattan breeze cooled her face if not her frustration. Wishing she hadn't lost her temper, she took a deep breath as she waved for a cab. She'd be regretting this night for months.

"Do you have the balls?"

Him. Why was he throwing her words back in her face?

Zoe looked into his eyes, surprised at how green they looked in the lamplight. Moss green. She said, "You want to wager that much? Yours'll be about two hundred gran. Grand." She teetered drunkenly.

He grabbed her shoulders to steady her. Through the cool evening, the heat of his hands infused her shirt. "Thanks," she said, stumbling into his chest. She stayed there.

"You're pretty good with numbers, Ice Queen. It took me half a beer to make that calculation."

"Did you call me *Ice Queen*?" Zoe tried to sound outraged, but Phillip had to be the only man alive who noticed more than her ass. If it took ice to survive Wall Street, then so be it.

"Everyone calls you that—hell, *you* probably call you that."

"Your point is?"

"You'll melt."

"Last guy didn't think so." Why was she having a heart-to-heart with Phillip?

"A neophyte."

Zoe heard inherent competence in his tone. Ah, that capability. Her drunken mind flashed an image of Phillip running his tongue along her inner thigh. Slowly.

Zoe blinked to clear the picture. "Uhh—" Why was she standing out here, pressed against this spectacular man? *Oh yeah, a cab.* "I need a cab." Then she looked up into his face from his chest and saw unresolved business. "I'm definitely bed—better than you." She thought she needed to qualify that. "My funs—funds are better."

She watched him suppress a smile. Those martinis were dragging her mind right into the gutter, and her mouth was happily following.

"Are you sure?" he asked. "You haven't heard the terms."

Zoe grabbed his arms to catch herself. She could feel how well muscled he was. She moved her hands up a little bit and found more muscles. She had to stop this. "I need—I need to—"

Zoe's vivid imagination flipped her a picture of exactly what she needed—Phillip's hand in her hair, his lips on her neck, her eyes closed in appreciation.

She cursed herself and the martinis. "I need to go home." She stepped away from him.

He stopped her, gently. "I don't want your money when I win."

Zoe stumbled again on her dratted shoes and pressed against his thigh. "What *do* you want?"

"You. I want you—as my sex slave."

"You didn't just say *sex slave*, did you?"

"Only if you don't get the promotion."

The vodka easily let her imagine granting his every sexual wish. Her heart raced, and her cheeks burned. Even if the idea were slightly appealing—and it wasn't—could Haas or anyone else ever work for her if they thought she slept around? "You've been reading *Hustler* too long."

"Who's going to get the promotion?"

"I am. And you know it."

"Take the bet."

"I'm not sleeping with you or anyone else from the office."

"So I'd have to quit the firm?"

"Pretty much." She staggered against him again and tried not to appreciate his masculine strength. "There's never a cab when you need one."

"What if we take the 'sex' part out?"

"Want a slave? Call a maid."

"No penetration."

"That's right. Not now. Not ever." The smell of him made her want to wrap herself in his sweater.

"What I mean, is that if I lose the bet, I fork over my bonus—a sizable sum as you've noted. If I win, you'll be my sex slave—with no penetration."

Zoe's head swam. She imagined his hand running the length of her body, an image so hot her mind skittered away from it. She then thought of the impassive New Englander and her new account. She couldn't lose.

"I'll do it," she heard herself say.

"Sign here." He thrust a napkin from the bar and a pen at her. The napkin was covered in tiny handwriting, and the letters jumped and danced as she squinted. Focusing through the alcohol was difficult, but she finally read, "If Zoe Lauterborn is promoted, I, Phillip T. Kingdom, will sign over my entire bonus to her. If I am promoted, Zoe Lauterborn will be my sex slave from seven P.M. until the following noon, beginning Friday, May twelfth. She must obey my every command." He had signed it on the bottom.

"My God, when did you write this?"

"When I knew you'd never let me take you on a regular date."

"You're right," Zoe laughed, knowing he'd just signed away two hundred grand.

"I didn't know your middle initial."

"Where's that pen?" Using a parking meter as a desk, she scrawled something. Then, ignoring the slickness between her thighs, she signed her name.

"I'll keep that," Phillip said, taking the napkin from her. He read it and grinned. "I like the additions. Are you going to tell me what 'L' stands for?"

"Lynn."

He folded the napkin and put it in his shirt pocket. Phillip held out his hand to her. His palm sizzled against hers.

Dear God, what have I done? Zoe wondered as a cab finally pulled up.

Running through Central Park early Saturday morning, Phillip wondered if he should feel guilty. Maybe sending her those martinis had been a bad idea. He'd never seen her drink more than a beer or glass of wine before last night—she'd probably have a hell of a hangover this morning. Poor baby.

"Poor baby, my ass," he said to himself, speeding up the hill past the Natural History Museum. She'd be mean as a hellcat and pissed off to boot. His sympathy would be wasted. Passing a college-age girl jogging with a giant poodle, he decided to absolve himself of any guilt. He hadn't poured the drinks down her throat. Not exactly.

Then Phillip grinned, remembering the way she'd pressed her thigh against his in the booth. Getting her drunk might have been worth it. And she definitely would have slapped him if she'd been sober when he handed her that napkin.

That napkin. His heart rate raced now, and not only from his punishing speed.

When Zoe remembered the napkin, she was really going to go ballistic. Maybe she'd been so drunk she'd forget about it. Slowing his pace around the pond, he considered crumpling it. Taking advantage of her rare bravado had been a dirty—if mouthwatering—trick. Tossing the napkin would be the gentlemanly thing to do.

Then he grinned in the spring air. He had Zoe Lauterborn's signature, and the world was his oyster.

On Friday at three, she took a deep breath and looked at the clock on her computer screen. Maybe the wager was a bad idea, but regret was for wimps. Abruptly the time registered in her brain, causing her stomach to flip. In fifteen minutes her win would be confirmed. Her New Englander had signed on Monday, and her ducks were in a row. Ten minutes ago her stocks had been outperforming Kingdom's by nearly two percent. No one else was even close.

She stood, planning a quick lipstick check, but a delicate caress along the nape of her neck stopped her in her tracks. Even as the delicious shiver traveled down her spine, she told herself it was only nerves.

"I can't wait to see your hair down."

"And I can't wait for that corner office."

"I bet," Phillip said with a grin.

The double meaning wasn't lost on her, but she couldn't return the volley. Today she would see years of effort—college, grad school, low-paying, tedious jobs—bear fruit. Today, she would earn her own department, fair and square. "You think you're very clever," she replied, lamely.

"I am. So are you. That's why this'll be fun even if I lose."

"*When* you lose," she corrected, and then, only half kidding, she asked, "Are you going to be able to take orders from me?"

"You'll be the one taking orders."

"You have a one-track mind, Kingdom."

He smiled. "Only where you're concerned."

She wished his eyes were the color of wet cement.

"Go manage your funds, Kingdom. The last I saw, they needed it." She strode off, taking heart from the bossy click of her high heels on the tile.

But when she walked into the conference room, she knew something was wrong. Moore wouldn't meet her eye.

"Zoe," he said, "I need to talk to you. Alone." Moore took her elbow and walked her out of the room.

He whisked her past the cubicles into his lair. He sat behind his mahogany desk and grunted.

"What is it?"

"I can't promote you."

Although not a muscle twitched in her face, the blood drained from it. *How was she going to face these guys?* She thought for sure she'd land this.

"But my—"

"I know. You're the best. You outperformed everyone in the division—by a lot."

Zoe looked through the glass door and saw Phillip Kingdom wink at her. Adrenaline raced down to her toes. *Oh my God. What exactly are the terms of that bet?* Her mind raced. Did her funds have to outperform his, or did she have to get the promotion? "You can't—"

"Sorry, Zoe. I would've advanced you, for the record, but the partners won't allow it."

Those bastards. "It's because I'm a woman. I'll sue," she said flatly.

"I wouldn't do that." Moore's tone was kind, not patronizing. "They think you're too . . . distant maybe. They think you don't have a good enough rapport with the other team members to lead."

They won't promote the Ice Queen. Zoe remembered the

endless happy hours she'd endured for the sake of team spirit, and the injustice of it made her want to howl.

Then she imagined Phillip pulling her hair out of its bun and actually moaned.

"It's not the end of the world. You're consistently good. Hell, I think you're the best here. Next year they'll *have* to move you into a lead position." Moore looked at his watch and stood. "We have to get to the meeting." He held the door for her, and they headed toward the conference room. "FYI, Kingdom's getting this one."

Zoe's stomach sunk.

Phillip watched her face when Moore announced the news. God, she was good. The muscles around her eyes tightened almost imperceptibly, but if hadn't known how much this meant to her, he would never have detected what must have been horror and disappointment.

Today, he felt like a fraud, and that thought surprised him. When she'd landed that huge account on Monday, they'd all been in awe, and he'd all but kissed that bonus away. Everyone in this room knew she deserved the promotion, but here he stood, shaking Moore's hand.

He was a rat.

"Congratulations," Moore said, still shaking his hand.

"Thank you, sir."

"Play nice, Phillip. Zoe's not far behind you."

"I hear you."

"FYI, management thought you were a better team player." So that was how they justified it. "I'll try to live up to it then."

"You do that." Moore walked away, leaving him shaking the hands of Haas then McMurtry and Thompson.

When Zoe came to congratulate him, he almost felt like he should apologize. The napkin, tucked into his pocket, felt like a lead weight. He's chuck it as soon as he got out of here.

"Congratulations," she said, meeting his gaze. He wanted to brush that tendril of hair back from her cheek, until she said, "You're officially a good ol' boy. Feel good?"

"Looking forward to tonight?" he lashed before he could think. *Damn my mouth.*

"Bastard," she replied so softly he could barely hear her. *Double damn.*

She washed her face in cold water, and went to hide in her cubby—which was not a corner office. The napkin was sitting on her desk, or at least a photocopy of it was. Without alcohol in her veins, the letters stood perfectly still. She read, "If Zoe Lauterborn is promoted . . ."

With a small cry, she crunched it up and tossed it away. Under it, a note said, "Wear something appropriate for Peter Luger's. Not a suit. Not pants." He'd also left a map to his home.

She picked up the phone and dialed his extension.

"Kingdom," he said.

"I'm going to sue you."

"No you won't."

"For sexual harassment."

"You agreed to it."

"You mean I signed it? Ha. You got me drunk. That's harassment, too."

"You got yourself drunk, and you did more than sign it. You amended it."

"What? My initial?"

"You weren't that drunk."

"I was so."

He laughed.

"How did I amend it?"

"You added three clauses. I could sue *you* for sexual harassment."

"You're crazy."

"Read what you wrote, Zoe L."

Zoe picked the crumpled sheet off the floor and read her own writing, "No pain. No pictures. No penetration." She gave a cry of dismay.

He didn't soothe her. "You'll regret the 'no penetration' part before the night's over." She could hear the grin in his voice.

"Creep." She slammed down the phone.

She was going to die.

3

At exactly seven o'clock, she rang the bell of his brownstone.

"Wow," he said, when he opened it. "A dress. You look great. Please, come in." As she walked past him, he caressed the small of her back. He watched her suppress a flinch. He'd need a slow hand tonight. But she'd definitely be worth it. "Black suits you. What is this?"

"Calvin Klein. Velveteen. A little spandex." She could barely speak, she was strung so tightly. Could he really blame her?

"It's okay. Breathe." He led her to the living room, and she followed silently.

"I made dinner reservations for seven forty-five. We have a few minutes. Here, sit down." Phillip waved her toward a leather couch. He watched her sit woodenly on the sofa as he headed toward the kitchen.

He brought back two glasses of red wine and handed one to her. "The way I see it, this is about control. You're so used to managing every little detail that you don't know when to let go."

"Thanks for the analysis." She didn't use the lighthearted tone that usually accompanied their banter.

He sat on the couch opposite her. "Ah, lighten up. You're probably terrified, but I'm not going to hurt you."

"I'm *not* terrified." He might have believed it, if her voice hadn't quavered.

"Have another sip of wine."

She did. So did he.

"Take off your panties." He paused then said, "Tonight you'll have no say. In anything."

"My—"

"No. Don't argue. You agreed to this. Now take them off."

Zoe took another deep drink and looked away from him. "How mortifying."

"Think of it as indulging one of my fantasies."

"A fantasy?"

"Knowing I can touch you any time I want to . . . yes, a fantasy." Explaining this to her ratcheted up his excitement, but Phillip squashed it, knowing self-control was his only hope for winning her over.

Zoe emptied her glass, set it on the table, and stood. He bet her knees trembled, and she looked extremely aware of his gaze. She reached demurely under her clingy dress, hooked her thumbs under the strings on her hips, and pulled down. The panties landed in a pink satin puddle around her feet. Zoe stepped delicately to one side and sat back on the sofa. She looked at him with a challenge in her eye.

Phillip walked over and picked them up. Holding them on one finger, he said, "Beautiful." Then he grinned and said, "But your ass will look better without them." He put them in his pocket and looked at her, appraisingly. "In fact, you look great without them."

"Thief."

"You'll give me everything I want."

"I want my underwear back."

"You just think you do." Phillip sat next to her. "Without them, you'll be thinking about sex all night." He put his hand on her thigh, on her inner thigh. "You'll be wondering how I'm going to touch you." Her muscles tightened, and ignoring her, he moved his hand a fraction higher. "And when I'm going to touch you." Phillip subtly stroked her leg—hinting that he might stroke higher, that he might venture under her dress. "Will I use my hand?" He gently squeezed. "Or my tongue?"

She sat very still, saying nothing.

"Is this so awful?" He continued the subtle caress.

"Yes," Zoe nearly whispered. "It's awful." She quivered under his touch.

"I think you're lying. How does it feel?"

"If I say 'throbbing' now, can I go home?"

"Give it up. You know you want to be here."

She didn't reply.

In a low and seductive voice, he continued, "Imagine feeling this way for the rest of the evening." She didn't meet his eye. "Whenever I brush against you, you'll think of my touch. You'll brush against me—perhaps accidentally, perhaps not— and you'll think of my touch. You'll be craving me by evening's end."

Still she said nothing.

Phillip bent to whisper in her ear. "I'll notice. You have a great ass, Zoe, even when it's under that Armani armor at the office. Dressed, or undressed, I won't be able to keep my eyes off you, and neither will anyone else."

A small moan escaped her.

"Tonight, you are all mine." He moved his hand again, pushing between her legs a little more, barely brushing her labia.

Pleasure corkscrewed in his stomach as she loosened her thighs just a bit. "Do you feel fearless yet?"

"Uh—I wouldn't describe myself as fearless right now."

"That gives us something to work on during dinner then."
He stood and held out one arm, indicating that she should pre-
cede him. He was dying to see the curve of her ass without
panties. But he wouldn't touch—not yet.

The four-star steak house was hip without being swanky—
the kind of place she usually enjoyed. Zoe breathed a sigh of relief. He couldn't humiliate her too much in a public place,
could he?

Despite the crowd and noise, Phillip procured a tiny booth
in the back. He ordered for both of them: red wine, salads,
medium-rare steaks.

"But what if I'm a vegetarian?" she asked, after the waiter
had gone. "Or hate blue cheese?"

"I watched you inhale a medium-rare burger last Friday," he
answered, toying with his water glass. "You like to dip your
fries in the blue cheese you order for your salad."

Zoe blinked, impressed he'd noticed these details. What did
she know about him? "I know you drink milk in your coffee,"
she offered.

"That's a start." He agilely fished an ice cube from his water
glass and handed it to her. "You'll know a lot more about me
before the night is through."

She took it, looking puzzled. His hand seemed especially
hot against the ice.

"Use it. Make your nipples hard."

Her face grew hot. "What? Here? Are you cr—"

"Do I need to show you what you signed? Besides," he
grinned, "no one's looking."

She looked around, hoping for some reprieve. "Don't look
while I do it," she begged.

"That would defeat the purpose," he laughed.

She'd be lying if she said she didn't think this was a little bit fun. Zoe took the melting cube and sucked the excess water from it, with her eyes locked on his. She slipped it under her dress and bra to her nipple. It instantly hardened, throbbing an erotic message right to her core.

"Now the other one." Phillip's voice sounded huskier than it had a moment ago.

Zoe groaned with the continued torture but switched hands. The tiny ice cube again sent an immediate zip to her clit. Zoe shifted so that her now throbbing sex wasn't pressed against the booth.

"How does it feel?" he asked.

"Embarrassing." She looked at the crowd, anywhere but at him. She dropped the remaining frozen bit to the floor.

"Besides that. Does it feel good?"

"Yes," she said, looking at him directly. What could he do to her right in the restaurant? "It reminds me of being in high school. It's the sort of thing I did when I was a kid."

"You mean, masturbate in public?"

"Not masturbate exactly . . ." Her voice trailed off. Why was she bringing this up?

"You're lucky you never sent anyone to jail."

"Who said I didn't?" she asked, and sipped her wine. "Maybe I'll send you to jail."

Phillip chuckled. "Not yet. Let's see you pinch your nipples."

"I don't think—"

"Slaves obey their masters, or they're punished."

"This is really going to your head," she said.

"Yes it is," he agreed.

She clenched her teeth and made to slip her hand into the top of her dress.

"No. From the outside. I want to see your fingers at work."

"But someone might—"

"I don't care if the whole world sees."

"I do," she said defiantly, but she gently worked her nipple between her thumb and middle finger. Her jaw loosened as the erotic sensation coursed through her, and she stifled a whimper as the hard bud easily peaked through the fabric of her bra and dress. She couldn't believe that this arrogant man could get such intense arousal from her.

"Do them both at the same time." His voice was so thick it almost growled.

This time she didn't balk before she obeyed him.

"Here you are, miss. Sir," said the waiter as he slid their meals in front of them. His expression appeared completely professional, and for a moment Zoe thought her little show had gone unnoticed. But a grin so quick she might have imagined it told her otherwise.

"I'm going to kill you when this is over," she snarled at Phillip after the waiter left.

4

Exiting the busy steak house, Phillip flagged a cab. As it pulled to a stop, he leaned over and whispered in her ear. "When was the last time you made out in the back of a car?"

Zoe didn't answer. Her heart pounded hard in her chest, and she became aware of the slipperiness between her thighs. The whole world must know she was turned on. She'd never played in a car before—not that she'd need to admit it to him.

"Please," he said, opening the car door for her. She slid in first, and loud free-form jazz accosted her ears. She couldn't hear Phillip's instructions to the cabbie. It wouldn't matter anyway. Her fate was in his hands. She leaned back feeling strangely relaxed. Maybe it was the wine.

The cab began to roll, and Phillip again put his hand high on her thigh. He grabbed her earlobe between his teeth and gently bit as he inched his hand up. As her clit lit up, she could almost imagine enjoying the surrender. "Take your bra off now."

"But—"

"The next time you say that word, I'm going to spank you. Now take it off."

S and M wasn't her style. She shut up.

Wearing a dress, she couldn't unhook the bra while sitting. "Could you please help me?" She leaned forward to give him access to her back.

"My pleasure," he said, sounding as if he meant it. With rough fingers, he traced her spine from the nape of her neck downward, and with a deft move, he unclasped it. His touch burned her skin. She pulled her arms into the dress and freed herself from the undergarment. He took the bra and ran it through his fingers.

"You've really surprised me. I would never have figured you for pink satin."

"Why not?"

"It's so obviously feminine. I'd have pegged you for black, or maybe dark purple."

"I'm pretty sure you just called me un-feminine."

"Are you kidding? You out-cat them all. But you keep it so tightly under wraps I'm surprised you own something like this." He stroked her neck with two fingertips and said, "And that you wore it tonight . . . I think you were feeling optimistic when you dressed."

"Funny. 'Optimistic' didn't cross my mind."

"You haven't even begun to know yourself yet." He put the bra in his pocket. "So, how does it feel to be braless?"

Reluctantly, she considered. The unfamiliar tug of gravity made her feel voluptuous. With a cup size that vacillated between A and B, 'voluptuous' wasn't a usual description for her. But she also felt naked, available to him.

"So how do you feel?"

She opted for the simple answer. "Bigger."

"And your nipples?" His tone was suggestive, making her aware of the fabric's texture brushing against them.

The context suddenly became sexual. "They're making me wet."

His hand dropped smoothly to the tip of her breast. Roughly, he caressed her. Even through the fabric, the temptation drew her. It felt sumptuous, opulent. Her nipple drew tight and eager.

She could almost imagine leaning back and letting him do what he wanted to her. And loving it.

"Hot," he murmured.

That was one way to describe it.

The cab pulled to a stop.

"Where are we?" she asked.

"The West Village. I thought we'd walk around a bit. Enjoy the spring night."

She stood on the curb while he paid the driver. The cool air between her hot thighs felt erotic, or maybe it was the press of her breasts against her dress. Her nipples were tight, no ice necessary. Couldn't everyone tell she was nearly naked?

"With an ass like yours, I've never noticed how great your breasts are. They look like they'd fit in wineglasses."

"I—I don't even know what to say to that."

"What about 'thank you?' "

"Thank you."

"That's a start." They began to stroll down the sidewalk. He'd taken her hand in his, and they probably looked like a normal couple to the people enjoying the outdoor bistros. "Now, give me a compliment. It has to be true."

"Umm . . ." She thought about his ass, and his eyes, about how good he was at his job. She thought about his wicked humor.

"Is it so hard to come up with one?"

"Yes."

Phillip looked at her, and she relented with the truth. "You asked for *one*."

He looked so relieved she had to laugh.

"What was the first that came to your mind?" he asked.

"I love looking at your ass, too. Do you know how many men have really ugly butts in suit pants? Not you."

"And you didn't go with that one because . . . ?"

She grinned, looking at his crotch, "I thought it might go to your head."

"Ah, Zoe," he pulled her closer and put his arm around her waist. "You've already gone to my head."

She stopped and looked up at him. "Can I ask you something?"

"I might not answer, but you can try."

"This is going to sound trite or blasé, but will you still respect me in the morning?"

"Lauterborn, you're as good as I am at our job. Hell, you're better. Nothing we do tonight will take that away from you. I will respect you in the morning," he enunciated the words very carefully. "And on Monday and until you get promoted out of my universe. And even then I'll still respect you."

"But—"

Glee lit up his face. "Now I get to spank you."

Horrorstruck, she realized what she'd said. "That's not fair! I didn't mean it. I won't say it again."

They started walking again. "Too late." His grin was impish, and he lowered his hand to the curve of her ass. He caressed it, promisingly, and it made her adrenaline course. But a small part of Zoe's brain found an appropriate ground for objection.

"No pain. Remember that part?"

"I won't hurt you . . . much. Don't object again," he warned in a good-humored tone. "I don't want to spend the *entire* evening with a paddle. There are so many other ways to have fun." His smile had turned wicked.

"No pain," she repeated, as much to comfort herself as to remind him.

"No pain," he agreed, pulling her tightly against him.

The warmth from his body comforted her.

As they walked past a small alley, he said, "This is just right."

"What is?"

He steered her toward the shadows and backed her against the wall. He caressed the side of her face with his hand. "So, you're standing in a dark alley with me, and you're not wearing anything under your dress. Are your feeling fearless yet?"

Before she could answer, he touched her top lip with his tongue, then eased across her bottom lip. She gasped and shivered but didn't move away. "I'm not afraid."

He pressed his lips fully against hers. She tentatively returned the kiss. His lips did not disappoint. They were hot and skilled, tender and moist. Under his, hers grew warmer and bolder.

He withdrew for a moment, just long enough to look closely at her face. Apparently he liked what he saw because he immediately took her lips again, harder and more possessively this time.

He touched her mouth with his tongue again, teasing and questing, until she shyly parted her lips, and she felt the intimacy of his tongue for the first time. Her hunger grew, and she returned his kisses with growing passion.

Then he took her wrists in his hand and held her arms above her head. She was completely at his mercy. As he pressed his hard-on against her, she moaned in pleasure. He moved his lips over her neck and up near her ear. His hand likewise roamed. The heat of it seared through her skin as he moved over her hip, up her stomach and to her breast.

"Still fearless?" he asked huskily.

She sighed and pressed against him.

"Answer me."

"Yes."

"Do you want more?"

Fire raced through her veins. She couldn't remember responding like this before. She hadn't known it'd been possible. "I want more."

Still pinning her arms above her, he brought his face to her breast. Pulling down her dress, he captured a tight nipple between his teeth and softly bit. His tongue circled it with hot, wet flicks, then slowed for an unhurried sampling swirl. She arched her back in pleasure, and he grabbed her breast with his free hand. He lifted it toward him, sucking harder and kneading, and a mewling sound escaped her. His teeth closed in another almost-bite, another flick of his skillful tongue.

She'd never felt as hungry for anything as she felt for him at that moment.

He pulled away and she moaned in dismay. "You like it, don't you?" he asked.

"Yes."

His lips closed briefly to suck and then opened again for another whirling attack.

She realized she was whimpering in pleasure and tried to stop.

His hand left her breast and traveled down her leg.

"Do you want me to stop?" Under her dress, his hand touched her bare thigh and she sharply gasped. She couldn't believe the searing heat. His hand inched higher and higher, and her heart pounded in her ears. So close.

"Do you want me to stop?" he asked, again. His fingers caressed her labia with a feather-light touch, nanometers from her clit. She thought she might die from desire, and she flexed her hips toward him.

"No. Please. I want more." Burning, she shifted to push herself against his hand, craving the relief of his touch.

He pulled his hand away as if he'd touched a flame. "I'm running the show tonight, Zoe—not you."

He released her arms, and he kissed her neck and ear as she groaned in consternation.

"I'm flattered that you want me and you trust me, but you must obey me. When I tell you that you can press against me, then you can. Or, if you really want something, you can ask. Nicely."

Zoe said, without any real fire, "You bastard."

"Maybe I'll relent, and maybe I won't."

"You're cruel," she said, collapsing limply into his arms.

"I'll make it up to you." The warmth of his stroking hands soothed her.

"This is mortifying."

"No, it's not." He petted her head and back. "You have to trust me."

She muttered something unintelligible, disgusted.

"Zoe?" he asked, his lips nuzzling her neck.

"What?"

"You're really hot."

"You're still a merciless man, Kingdom."

5

A half-moon hung over them as they walked through the streets. Bass thumped out of clubs, reverberating through Phillip's shoes. At a quieter club with a purple and yellow sign, he said, "Henrietta's. Let's go in."

He paid the cover and escorted Zoe to the bar. "A beer—whatever's on tap—and a strawberry daiquiri," he said to the bartender.

"I didn't know you liked daiquiris, Phillip," she said wryly, apparently still miffed at being denied. Phillip felt like the luckiest man in the world—the way she responded to him took his breath away. But even Phillip knew he could ratchet up her desire—by forbidding it.

"Pink suits you, even when you're annoyed."

"Who's annoyed? I just don't drink daiquiris."

"Don't you like rum? Strawberries?"

"Anything that comes with an umbrella is too . . ."

"Feminine?"

She laughed, and he knew he had her pegged.

"Froufrou," she corrected.

"Not everything feminine is froufrou."

"For example?"

"Like your hair, for instance." Phillip reached over and pulled it out of its loose bun. It fell around her face. "Blond silk," he noted. "I should have done that in the restaurant," he said appreciatively. He ran his fingers through it, and she shivered. "Looking at you this way, I can't decide whether you look like Rachel Hunter or Heidi Klum."

The bartender, a thick woman, brought them their drinks. With a knowing grin, she gave the beer to Zoe and the daiquiri to Phillip. "Keep him in line, girlfriend," she said after she collected the cash.

Tolerantly, Phillip switched the drinks back with a grin.

As Zoe sipped the strawberry concoction, which tasted surprisingly good, she looked around the bar. The music was less frenetic than the other clubs they'd passed, and a few people danced. They were all women. In fact, Phillip was one of only three men in the place.

He watched her face, waiting for the implication to sink in. His wicked smile let her know he'd picked this place with her in mind. "Yup," he said quietly to her, "it's a girl bar. Now go dance."

"With you." The pleading look almost made him relent.

"I'm flattered you'd ask." *But you're going alone*, his tone implied.

"Please?"

"They won't bite. I want to watch. Consider it payback. I know you watched me last weekend." He touched her long hair.

She didn't deny it, and she answered, "Give me my bra back."

"No way. And I'm giving the orders."

"My underwear? Please?"

"No. Go."

"God, can I at least put my hair back up?" she asked desperately.

"Nope."

"But it's like I'm ready for bed."

"I'm getting you ready to bed," he agreed.

"I mean, it's like I'm in my pajamas!"

"You said 'but,' Zoe. I should count that when I spank you."

"She went to the dance floor.

Oh my God, he was a lucky man.

The music had a great beat, and she liked to dance—or she had liked to dance when she was younger. After a song or two, she warmed to the idea, and her hips and heels easily found the rhythm. Women danced with each other and floated away. Some, like her, danced by themselves. Occasionally a man braved the dance floor, usually with a woman. But Phillip stayed by the bar, watching her with an intimidating intensity.

A slender, graceful woman with long dark hair danced with her for a while. They provided good foils for each other, her long dark hair giving the perfect counterpoint to Zoe's blond. Zoe lost herself trying to complement the other woman's movements. One song melted into another before Zoe realized they were monopolizing the dance floor. How could she have let such a simple pleasure escape her life?

After the exertion of several more songs, Zoe excused herself. She was thirsty.

As she walked toward Phillip, she saw desire in his eyes. Suddenly, she felt very, very sexy. With her eyes half closed, she let her hips, loose from dancing, sway with each stride.

Zoe sipped the strawberry concoction through the straw, savoring the icy chips. Acutely aware of Phillip's attention, she was too shy to meet his eye.

Phillip said in a husky voice. "I had no idea you could dance like that."

"It's been a long time," she admitted. "High school, maybe?"

"My God, I wish I'd known you in high school." He groaned and said, "Maybe it's a good thing I didn't know you then."

"I'm glad you're the tortured one for a change," she said with a half smile.

"You could really torment me, if you set your mind to it."

"You'd deserve it," she said, meaning it.

"Stand in front of me and look at the dance floor."

She did.

"Give me your hand." With her back toward him, she reached behind herself.

He took her hand and put it on his hard-on. It was huge and hot and shockingly hard. She gasped in surprise—and brazenly moved in closer to him. She'd get some revenge.

"This is what you do to me," he said, his voice thick.

His blatant desire sent a jolt right between her thighs. For the first time since she signed the napkin, the night seemed rich with potential and promise. With the music's rhythm still in her blood, she began to move to the beat.

Remembering the alley, she didn't dare take matters too much into her own hands. "Do you want me to stop?" she asked over her shoulder, coyly.

"No." His reply was clipped. Zoe knew he was focused on controlling himself, and her confidence grew.

Teasing him, Zoe made sure her ass bumped his thighs with each throb through the sound system. Then she released him and turned toward him, bobbing gently to the bass. She could feel her breasts bouncing on the counter beat, and arousal tightened low in her belly.

"Keep dancing for me," Phillip said, his voice a velvet drawl.

She took a step away so he could see her better. In a private show just for him, she swung her hips to the beat and thrust her pelvis a little bit. She was in the groove and hit each move just right.

"My God," he murmured, "the way you push it." His smoldering look gave her confidence, made her glow. He rested his hands on her waist, and with every bop of her hips Zoe became increasingly aware of her every curve. She danced to provoke him—twisting to bring his thumb closer to her breast, turning to run his hand over her flat stomach, moving so his fingertips floated over her ass.

He stood and began to dance with her. He didn't overpower her. Instead, he brushed against her, teasing back and inviting. A caress here. A stroke there. She seductively turned, and his lightest touch told her that she had his complete attention.

The music slowed, and he took her into his arms. He didn't press against her, but she grew extremely aware of his presence. His hooded eyes had darkened, and they never left her. She knew if she touched him between his legs, she'd find him rock hard, and she felt powerful. Electricity sparked between them. When her breast touched his chest, her nipples instantly hardened, and her desire for him became almost palpable.

"We're going," he almost groaned.

Zoe didn't object.

They were breathing hard when they left the club, not just from physical exertion. Phillip led them around a corner toward Washington Square Park. A fountain spouted sparkling water toward the sky. A vast garden of daffodils surrounded the fountain with a yellow so bright she could see them in the moonlight.

"Beautiful," Zoe remarked.

"Yes. Let's walk around it." He set a slow, leisurely pace. Night shrouded the park in mystery. The dog run, usually roiling with canine life and yuppy owners, stood gray and empty, and she saw none of the usual clean-cut NYU students playing frisbee or hanging out.

Zoe caught a whiff of marijuana as they passed several couples sitting on iron benches. Most were making out. Zoe saw someone giving head to someone else, and she quickly looked away, trying not to feel scandalized. Phillip slowed the pace further, and her heart began to pound. She jumped nearly out of her skin when a car alarm went off right behind her. The bright lights of Broadway seemed miles rather than steps away.

"Here," he said finally, leading them to an empty bench. "Let's catch our breath."

That sounded innocent enough. Zoe sat, and he moved in next to her. The cold iron of the bench quickly permeated her dress and chilled her heat. She shifted back to avoid it. "Are you cold?" he asked, moving closer still.

"If you'd've asked me yesterday, the answer might have been different," she said with a brave grin.

"You were never cold—you just needed . . ."

"What? You?" She challenged.

"A firm hand. Show me your breast."

She bridled, but then checked herself. Maybe he'd forget the spanking thing if she were obedient from here on out. Subduing her embarrassment, she pulled the front of her dress until her breast was bared to the cool night air.

And to his mouth. He leaned over and licked it. She could feel his hot breath on the wet, sensitive skin. The sensations bewitched her senses.

"Hold it for me, Zoe. Hold your breast."

Shutting out all other thoughts—like that someone might see them, that good girls don't hold their own breasts or make out in parks—she cupped her breast and offered it to him.

He devoured it, roughly caressing her back, her arms. He surrounded her with his touch as he ravaged her.

Slowly, images from the intimidating park melted away, leaving her with a growing awareness of him—his teeth, his tongue, his fingers and palms. She shivered at the sensation running through her, the deep throbbing desire that made her ache for him. Almost against her will she moved against him, wanting more. She grew increasingly willing to accept whatever he would give.

She arched her back in pleasure.

"Relax, Zoe. Lean your head back and enjoy the ride."

She did as he said, basking in the strange sense of freedom. A long sound of pleasure escaped her. It was loud enough so that at the least the people on the nearest benches must have heard her. She didn't care.

He flicked his tongue across a taut nipple, and she shuddered in pleasure. Her delight grew. She squirmed in his arms, gasping. "Please," she said, begging for release. His hand crept up her bare thigh, and she felt only anticipation, excitement.

Finally, finally, he reached between her legs and oh so gently stroked her.

His mouth traveled up to the tender spot behind her ear. He bit her earlobe as his fingers slipped over and around her throbbing clit.

She fought back a moan and the urge to press against him. Enslaved by the delicious ravishment that overwhelmed her senses, Zoe yielded herself completely. If he stopped now . . .

"Ohh," she moaned, widening her legs. "Don't stop."

He didn't.

She couldn't control herself any longer. Zoe began moving rhythmically against his hand and shifting to show him exactly the right angle. She hadn't known the angle would matter. *Here?* he seemed to ask. *No, there. Like this? Yes, just like that.*

He added more fingers. Suddenly it felt like he had a fingertip slithering around every slippery centimeter.

Her body stiffened and she knew she was so close. He didn't miss a beat. Suddenly, she cried out. She knew everyone in the park heard her, and she didn't care a bit. Her muscles pulsated against his fingers, and he expertly pressed against her, satisfying her.

Finally, she fell against him in exhaustion.

"Is it always that good?" she nearly whispered a few minutes later, still basking in the radiant feeling of it.

"It should be."

His thick voice reminded her that he'd had no such release.

"Can I—can I do something for you?" She moved her hand, slightly, to clarify her offer.

"Yes," he said, moving her hand away from him. "Tell me how long it's been since someone did that for you."

"You mean, take my underclothes, make me dance nearly naked in front of a bunch of lesbians, and then maul me in a public place?" she asked, laughing.

"I want an answer," he said in a warning voice.

"Do you mean, when was the last time someone touched me?" she asked in a more serious tone.

"No. When was the last time someone made you come?"

Her shoulder muscles tensed defensively. He must have felt it, because he said, "It's nothing to be ashamed of."

"I guess Jeff and I weren't all that compatible. Sexually."

"How long were you together?"

"Close to two years."

"You spent two years with someone who didn't satisfy you?"

"Well," she said, trying not to sound self-protective. "He used to try."

"Do you mean that you never once came with him?"

"Or with anyone else. It wasn't just him." She swallowed. "I thought orgasms—at least for women—were created for somebody's ad campaign. To sell cars and perfume."

"Do you still think that?"

"Having had one," she said, snuggling against him, "I believe that they're at least occasionally possible. But we didn't have sex, did we?" The question was rhetorical.

He admonished, "You should have them regularly."

"Once is one thing," she laughed. "I don't want to be greedy."

6

"There's a coffee house about two blocks from here," Phillip said, helping Zoe to her feet.

"At this hour?"

"You weren't planning on sleeping tonight, were you?"

She had been, actually. "Uh—" She swallowed, reminding herself to obey him.

Phillip took her hand. While they walked quietly for a few minutes, Zoe grew increasingly uncomfortable. God, what a scene she'd made. And who were the other people out there? Prostitutes? Junkies?

"Here we are," Phillip said. He found a table and ordered two mocha lattes with extra whipped cream.

The waiter walked away and Zoe said, "What if I were a tea drinker? Or what if I hated whipped cream?" Even she was surprised at the anger in her voice.

He said, calmly. "I see you drinking coffee at every meeting. I know you take both cream and sugar. A lot of sugar. A little cream."

She blinked. He was right.

"I watch which funds you buy, which you sell. I notice the colors of your clothes. How come you never wear blue, by the way? It'd look good on you. I know you like working with Thompson but not with Haas, and I know Moore really likes you."

"I hate whipped cream," she insisted, not mollified.

"You hate the *idea* of whipped cream." He dipped his finger into his drink and proffered it. "Try it."

Sex slave. She had to. She delicately licked the tiniest bit from his fingertip.

"You need to taste more than that." His whipped cream-dipped finger remained out.

This time, she sucked the whole thing off. Ignoring the heat growing in his eyes, she savored it while it melted over her tongue into a creamy mass. Damn him. It was good. So was the texture of his rough fingertip on her tongue.

"That's not the point," Zoe said, stubbornly. "You don't ask me what I like. I feel like—like—I don't know . . . a sexual object. Like I'm the leading porn star in some teenaged dream of yours."

"Porn stars generally get fucked. You have not been fucked."

"As Clinton said, 'It depends on what the definition of "is" is,' " she said, bitingly.

He wore a dark expression. "I won't fuck you. In either the literal or figurative sense." She saw him smooth his frown, and he took her hand in his, stroking it. In a softer tone, he said, "I never expected to win the bet."

"What?" She was confused by the apparent change of subject.

"Oh, come on. Your funds outperform mine most of the time."

"Usually not by much. Why'd you do it? Two hundred grand's a lot of money."

"I would've risked twice that for a night with you."

She dismissed that disdainfully. "Hmmf. Your *Penthouse* visions."

"Oh hell, you don't make this easy. What I mean is that I've been dying to take you out."

"Well, a normal guy would just ask."

"You would have said 'no' to a normal guy."

"That's—"

"Completely true," he interrupted. "I see how you cope. It can't be easy being one of four women among a hundred men. You don't date, so you don't have to deal with it."

"I go out with you guys," she said defensively. "To the happy hours and things."

"Why didn't you get the promotion?"

Because I'm the Ice Queen. She looked at her mug and didn't answer.

"If you had really surprised me and accepted a conventional dinner invitation, you would have kept your distance."

"How do you know?" she challenged. "I thought you were attractive. I might have fallen head over heels." She saw his look and added, "It could happen." She sounded defensive, even to herself.

"You would have worn ugly underwear and wondered why you felt so empty."

Again Zoe said nothing. That's exactly how she felt in the bar the night she got sloshed. She'd been jealous of the woman dancing with Phillip.

"I'm guessing that you feel humiliated for letting yourself go in the park."

She looked away from him, not denying it.

"Don't be."

"Easy for you to say. You're wearing all your clothes." She saw him smile at her lame joke.

"The fact that you came leaves me humbled."

She scanned his face and saw sincerity.

"I mean it. Even if all I get out of this is a bunch of hot images of you and the knowledge that you trusted me enough to cut loose, I'm a pretty lucky guy." Then he grinned and looked at his crotch, "A sore guy. But a lucky one."

"What if you'd lost all that money?"

"At least you would've noticed me," he shrugged. "I wouldn't have been just another guy politely asking you out only to get politely refused." He grinned at her, "I would have gone down in flames."

She conceded with a small laugh.

"Zoe?"

She looked at him.

"I'm really glad you're here with me tonight."

Maybe she was glad, too.

"What are you thinking?" he asked.

"I was wondering what an orgasm would feel like with you inside me."

"You have no idea how sexy you are."

"Would it feel different?" she persisted. She watched desire darken his eyes, and she felt a tiny bit of sympathy for him.

"Ah, but the clause you put into the bet . . ."

"You just said 'but.' Do I get to spank you?"

"Give a girl an orgasm and she thinks the world's her oyster. You're moving mighty fast, Ms. Lauterborn, and you're changing the subject."

"You just don't want to get spanked," she taunted him.

He kept his focus. "*You* said, 'no penetration.' " A look of mock sorrow crossed his face as he said, "So I guess you won't find out what your orgasm feels like."

"The way this night is going, you'll suffer more for it than I will," she replied flippantly.

"You have an evil sense of humor."

"I could've taken lessons from you."

"And you're a smartass."

"I thought you liked my ass."

"I love your ass."

That comment sent her heart to her throat.

Phillip walked them down a handful of blocks, and he stopped in front of a small shop bearing a bright pink neon sign.

"The 'Pink PussyCat?' " she read doubtfully.

"Don't say 'but.' " She heard his smile.

He led her down the stairs into the shop.

"It's—it's filled with sex toys," she whispered to him.

"Shh," he whispered back. "Don't let everyone know."

They walked past some frightening paraphernalia—executioner's masks, whips, paddles. She suddenly thought he was going to make good on his threat right here. Her stomach flipped at the thought. "No pain," she reminded him.

"Don't worry, Zoe. Breathe. The paddles are for the second date."

She gasped, and he looked at her. Whatever he saw made him merciful.

"I'm kidding. We're not here for the whips, or paddles, or chains. Come on." He pulled her forward.

She spied handcuffs and brightly colored things that she couldn't imagine uses for. Despite his reassurances, breathing became more difficult. Under duress, she might admit that the night had been . . . interesting, not nearly as demeaning as she'd anticipated. Surely he wouldn't take this too far now.

He escorted them past videos. She tried not to look too closely, but signs reading GIRL/GIRL and GUY/GUY and ORGIES caught her attention. The covers depicted a lot of naked and nearly naked people. Zoe really wanted her underwear back.

He finally stopped by a selection of oils. Oil seemed innocuous enough. Brown bottles with labels like "jasmine," "almond," and "patchouli," lined the counter. They had graceful lines, and he handed her one with a "vanilla" label. "How's it smell?"

She sniffed. "Good. But . . . too much like cookies." She put it down.

He picked up another, sniffed and grimaced. "What do you think?"

It was labeled "lavender." She sniffed. "Ugh. It smells like granny's living room. Who'd want that?"

"Maybe whoever it is that buys the executioner's masks," he said.

She laughed, relaxing a bit. "What about this?" She handed him a bottle.

"Mmm. This is what we're looking for. What is it? Essence of unicorn?" He looked at the bottle's front. "Oh, cinnamon. It matches you perfectly."

"Did we come here just for oil?"

Phillip laughed. "Don't sound so hopeful."

"You're not the one going commando."

He laughed again. "I'll protect your sweet bare ass from anything that might bite it."

"Including you?" She was not reassured. "Can we leave now?"

He took a fresh bottle of cinnamon oil from the shelf and said, "I think we need to look around some more."

He put his hand on her waist and pushed her toward a glass case. Vibrators and dildos of amazing colors and shapes filled it.

"Oh," she said doubtfully. "I don't think I'm ready for this." Then she found a lifeline. "And 'no penetration.' Remember? We can't use anything here."

"Who says a vibrator has to penetrate?"

"Don't they?" she said uncertainly.

"But these aren't what I'm looking for."

"They're not?"

"No. Do you want underwear?"

God knew what kind they sold here. "I want *my* underwear."

"Can I help you?" The woman behind the counter wore

black and hot-pink motorcycle gear, and her hair looked like Elvira's.

Zoe looked away, making it clear that the only help she needed was with the nearest exit.

"Do you carry 'The Butterfly?' " Phillip asked her.

"The one with the remote?"

"That's it."

"It's over here." She guided them toward the scary rack of unidentifiable stuff they'd passed on the way in. "We have it in pink and . . . let's see . . . purple."

"Pink, definitely."

"You're getting predictable, Kingdom," said Zoe quietly.

"Can I help you find anything else?" Elvira-hair asked.

"This'll do."

As they walked to the cash register, Phillip handed the item to Zoe. It didn't look frightening. The flat pink wings spanned maybe two inches, and it looked like it was made of soft latex. The package also had a small black box, not attached to the butterfly. She put it on the counter next to the oil.

"Do you want a battery?" asked Elvira-hair.

"Definitely," he answered.

Battery? What did it need a battery for?

"Here," he said, handing her the oil while he fumbled with the butterfly and battery. "This is hard to do while walking."

"Then don't." She aimed for nonchalant, but it came out worried.

"It's worth the effort." He smiled in amusement. "You'll agree with me in a few minutes."

He handed it to her. She saw that black satin bands ran behind the butterfly. "What is it?"

"Your new panties."

She could suddenly see how to wear it. Behind the butterfly was a smallish nub. It would rest right on her clit.

"Oh."

"Put it on."

Curious, she stopped in the shadow of a quiet building and slipped it on.

"Let me adjust that for you."

"Always the gentleman," she said, glibly. But when his palm covered her pubis and adjusted the butterfly, she gasped at the electrical intensity from him.

"Let's walk a bit."

The weight against her sex felt unfamiliar but not uncomfortable. She wasn't sure what its point was, but she tried to keep an open mind. "It's kind of interesting," she ventured, as they passed a crowded bar.

"We're going in."

Again, she had no choice.

She preceded him into the club and felt the eyes of the other customers fall on her. The heavy weight of her breasts registered in her mind, and just as she started to cross her arms over them, the butterfly vibrated. It felt like a thousand tiny fingers or tongues caressing her clit at once. The purely erotic shock of it nearly stopped her.

Phillip gently propelled her forward, toward the bar. He whispered, "Now you know how I feel when I look at you. You send a shock right to my cock."

The vibrating stopped.

"How—how did you do that?"

He held up the small black box she'd seen in the package. "Remote control," he grinned. "I can touch you—in a crowd, on the street—in the most private way, and only you and I know."

"You—"

He looked at her face and kissed her. Hot. Possessive. Adrenaline coursed through even her tiniest vein as her tongue met his. The novelty of their intimacy made her aware of his scent, the location of each finger on her back, her ass. She pressed against him, and the butterfly fluttered again. She sharply inhaled.

"Let's dance."

Like she had a choice.

Like she wanted one.

He led her to the packed floor, and as they danced, only inches separated them. The throbbing music permeated her every cell. He pressed against her breast, and she pressed back in pleasure. She grew bolder and moved her hip against his groin. He responded, lightly pinching her nipple and releasing it before she could draw a breath. In the packed room no one could see.

A space opened and she twirled. She found herself dancing with a stranger. He had a blunt, snubbed nose and a baby face. Phillip danced with a leggy redhead. She and the stranger danced well together, and Zoe tried to tell herself that Phillip's redhead was clumsy—it wasn't true.

The butterfly buzzed again, and Phillip's arms enveloped her. He surrounded her. The vibration stopped. "You're devious," she said in his ear.

"It's growing on you."

"Something's growing," she said, pressing against his erection. "And your butterfly's getting buttery."

"Between your legs, I'm surprised it's not melting."

"I'm melting."

"Hello, Zoe. Good-bye, Ice Queen."

The music slowed, and he pulled her fully against him. Her breasts pressed tightly against his chest, his arms were around her waist, his hands on her ass. She could feel his erection between her thighs. As she put her arms around him, he bent his head down and began to nibble her ear. The moment felt surreal. Surrounded by people, she felt totally alone with him. She felt like she was part of him.

When the butterfly began to flutter again, she whimpered, but only he heard it.

"I've got you," he whispered in her ear. And he did. The pad of his thumb caressed the outermost edge of her breast, and Zoe felt the burning pulse between her thighs grow. When he captured her lips in his, he took her breath away. Every last inch of her seemed to belong to him. In front of all the other dancers, she came. Violently. If she hadn't been in his arms, she would have crumpled on the dance floor.

"I've got you," he repeated.

7

Propped against him in the cab, Zoe supposed she ought to feel anxious. They were going back to his place. They'd be alone. There'd be a bed.

But she'd learned a lot about Phillip Kingdom in the last few hours, and some of those things surprised her. She'd thought he'd be arrogant. Instead he treated her kindly, respectfully. He'd opened doors for her that she'd thought had no keys, and he did it while leaving her spirit unbruised. No, she didn't feel nervous. If she were honest with herself, she felt excited.

Her put his arm around her, and pulled her in closer to him. "It'll take a few minutes to get home. Why don't you close your eyes?"

Comfortable. Inhaling his masculine scent, she drifted to sleep.

In what seemed like a heartbeat later, they arrived at his brownstone. Groggily, she followed him up the steps. He unlocked the door, put the oil and butterfly on an end table and flicked on the light. He gently ushered her to the living room.

"Here. Sit down. Are you hungry? Thirsty?"

"No. Sweaty. Stinky. I smell like cigarettes."

"That last club was pretty thick."

"And I'm all . . . sticky."

He chuckled. "That's not a bad thing. Wait here."

He disappeared into the kitchen, and this time, she noticed his décor. Maple floors. A thick wool rug with a Southwestern design. Stone fireplace. Nice.

"This place really captures your personality," she said when he returned.

"What do you mean?"

"Rugged. Masculine."

"I'm so rugged. Herbal tea?"

She laughed as he handed her a steaming mug.

"Oh, that's good," she said, after a cautious taste. "We kind of went on the alcoholic tour of the city tonight."

"I think the booze was secondary. Or maybe tertiary."

"Can you spell that?"

"Not with you sitting in front of me."

She ran her hand self-consciously through her hair.

"No, really. You look like a wild mountain pony."

She laughed, but his mood had intensified.

"Lean back, Zoe, and give me that 'come hither' look."

Still playful, she lounged into the corner of his sofa, half closed her eyes, and she licked her lips. "Like this?"

"Oh God yes, like that. Rachel Hunter. Not Heidi. Poor Heidi doesn't hold a candle to you."

"Oh please. She's a supermodel."

"Let go of your knees." She'd had her hands clasped in front of them, but she released them. Suspecting she knew where this was going, edgy excitement expanded in her belly.

"Pull up your dress, just a little. I want a peak."

She inched it up, swallowing her pride.

"A little more."

She did.

"You are so beautiful. Spread your legs, just a little."

"This is—"

"Breathtaking. Spread them more."

She widened her knees a smidge.

"Zoe." Disappointed.

She opened them more. "Phillip—"

"Shh. How can you object? I'm not even touching you."

Her sex must have glistened with the slippery wetness since each command torpedoed her clit with excitement. She felt like she was under a magnifying glass—that he could see her entire self. Disconcerting as that was, her belly tightened further with desire.

"Look me in the eye and stroke yourself. Show me how you like it."

"I don't *know* what I like."

"Then discover it."

She reached down to touch the delicate vee of soft curls, and with her other hand, she spread her labia with two fingers.

She heard him moan and moaned herself.

Glide.

Had she ever been this wet? Surely her clit had never been this swollen. Hot. Wet.

She didn't get far into her exploration. "I can't stand it—I can't keep my hands off you." Phillip crossed the room in two great strides and buried his face between her legs. She gasped and quickly removed her hand, but he grasped it and mumbled, "You do this, too."

His tongue ran the length of her and accompanied her fingers as they circled around her clit. He sucked carefully on her clit, and flicked his tongue. She couldn't tell which sensations were caused by him and which by her.

His hands reached up to find her breasts. Rough fingers caught her nipples, pinched and rolled them into hard, tingling tips.

A sudden hard suck brought her to the brink. She flexed her hips toward him, unable—no, unwilling—to hold back one more second. He sucked again—and she saw stars, fireworks, explosions.

She felt her muscles throb and pulsate, reaching for something that wasn't there. She gasped at the intensity, amazed at her body.

She fell back into the sofa, stroking his hair. He climbed completely onto the sofa, leaving his head on her lap. Within moments she was asleep.

Brilliant golden light filled the unfamiliar room, and Zoe woke to the feel of Phillip's muscled chest pillowing her head and the repetitive stroking of his hand on her hair. Soothing. She felt safe. He must have carried her upstairs last night.

His hot erection throbbed against her hip, distracting her. She blinked in the morning sunshine, surprised at the heat flooding through her.

"I thought moonlight really became you, but you look great in the sunshine, too." Arousal roughened his voice to a husky velvet drawl.

He flexed his powerful body, and Zoe could see just how well-muscled he was. Could she really have spent last night like she did and never have seen his chest? He was long and lean, that she'd known. But his thighs and arms and pecs looked like those of a cyclist or diver. Or a fencer. Gorgeous.

He moved, and she found herself underneath him. She blinked as he loomed above her, staring into her face. The urgent lust she'd seen throughout the night now mingled with something else. Tenderness? Affection? She blinked again.

Lifting a hand, Phillip gently drew it through her hair, combing the strands over the pillow. His absorbed gaze flicked over her hair and then rested again on her face.

"Before last night, I had no idea your hair was this long."

He definitely had a tender expression, and Zoe felt her stomach spiral. She stroked his chest, wordlessly.

"The bathroom's over there," he said, rolling off her and the bed.

Reality check. "I, um—I forgot to bring overnight things." It wasn't the sort of thing that would normally slip her mind. "I guess I was nervous."

"Don't worry. I've got you covered."

"Uncovered?"

"We'll get to that."

The promise sent a chill through her. It was a good chill.

"I bought a toothbrush for you. It's on the counter in there."

"Pink?" She sat on the edge of the bed rubbing her eyes.

He chuckled. "Of course."

"I wouldn't have thought you so predictable, Kingdom."

"I'm full of surprises."

"Ha, ha." Facing him, she stood and stretched, raising her arms high above her and arching her back. "Predictably full of surprises."

"You're quite the tease this morning."

"I learned from the master. Where'd you say the bathroom was?"

"Over there," he pointed. "Are you a size seven?"

"Yes."

"Good. I bought the right size."

"You planned this better than I did." The fact that he bought clothes for her last week made her feel . . . well, she didn't know how she felt. It was strange to know that he'd been thinking about such personal details.

"I can be an optimist, too," he said, staring at her ass.

* * *

The jade and copper bath complemented him as well as the living room did. The man had great taste. Zoe started the water running in the oversized shower and brushed her teeth. Waiting for the water to get hot, she looked in the mirror. She looked different. She looked again. What was it?

Then she realized . . . it'd been a long time since she'd seen her own smile in the mirror.

She stepped into the steaming water and let it sluice over her back. God, it felt good. She rolled her head one way and then the other. Just as she reached for the soap, she heard the door open.

"You a breakfast person, Zoe?"

"Depends what's on the menu."

"Great," he said, entering the bathroom and closing the door behind him. "I am." Seconds later he was in the shower with her. He took the soap from her and began to wash her back.

"You got pretty dirty last night." Erotic tension laced his voice. He slid his sudsy hands over her ass and down her thighs.

"I only followed your lead." No trace of guilt in her tone.

He slid over her calves and over that soft spot behind her knees. Had anyone ever touched her there before? "Mmm. That feels great."

He took the shampoo from the shelf, poured some in his hand, and lathered her hair. Gently, competently, like she was a child. He positioned her under the nozzle and carefully rinsed her hair, taking care to keep the soap from her eyes. It made Zoe feel . . . what? Cherished. She'd never had anyone wash her hair before, outside of the salon.

"Turn around." Husky. Thick.

Glycerin masked the roughness of his palms as he glided

around her neck, over her stomach, over her breasts. He spent long moments on them, slithering over one nipple and then the other. Within seconds, she was ready for him. "Oh, Phillip. You feel so good."

She couldn't take her eyes off his huge erection, imagining the heat of it under her lathered hand. He pressed a nipple and it sprang to attention. She let out another moan of desire.

"Isn't my time with you up yet?"

"You don't feel like you're in a hurry to leave." He slithered a hand between her thighs and grinned as she gasped. "You're still mine for a while."

He kissed her then, a hot and wicked kiss. Which she returned with a wickedness of her own. Breathless, she took the soap from him. "Can I wash you?"

"Not until the third date," he answered with husky humor. "Until noon you have to obey me. Now hold still."

He grabbed shaving cream from the shelf.

She thought of his face between her thighs. "How courteous of you."

"This isn't for me—it's for you. I already shaved."

Her? She didn't need a shave. "I don't un—"

He lathered the nest between her legs, and suddenly she understood. She'd thought he was through with the orders and commands. "Do you really need to do this?"

"Hold still," he said, positioning the razor as he kneeled before her. "I need a steady hand, and you have a way of making me shake."

He made her tremble, too.

The first slide of the razor felt cold, and on the second slide, he let his pinky glide over her clit. "Wait," she said. "I don't want to fall." She carefully shifted her legs farther apart.

He groaned appreciatively and said, "You like this."

"Conceited thing. The floor is slippery."

He flicked his tongue quickly over her clit, and said, "You're slippery." He shaved another swath and said, "Tell the truth. Did you move your legs apart because you want me?"

"Maybe."

"God, I hope so," he said, burying his face.

8

Out of the shower, he toweled her dry, patting her carefully from ankles to ears. "Put your hair up, please."

She twisted it back into a damp bun. Raising her arms, she saw his gaze grow hot as he watched her breasts. A pleasurable feeling of power coursed through her—he wanted her, she wanted him. She couldn't wait to discover what erotic adventure he had planned this time. He'd barely touched her, and yet she ached for him.

She realized that at some point during the evening, her brain had shifted gears. She no longer felt like an object of his lust. She didn't feel used—she felt like a partner in delicious, beautiful crime.

"Come back into the bedroom." She followed him, sauntering, and he positioned her a few feet from a full-length mirror. He had slipped on a pair of red silk boxers.

"Wait here. You can touch yourself, if you want." *Yeah, right.* She heard him step downstairs. She looked at her shaved area and was surprised to see that her clit actually peaked out. The haircut made her whole body look different, thinner somehow. She ran her palm over the bald patch. Her clit was so much more easily available, inviting a touch, a suck.

"I knew you couldn't keep your hands off yourself." He sounded pleased with himself.

She whipped her finger off her clit, but it was too late. She pushed her mild embarrassment to the far back of her mind. "You snuck up those stairs, didn't you?"

"Don't feel badly. I can't keep my hands off you either."

"Hmmh." The playful look in her eye belied her annoyed reply.

He shrugged, grinning. "I needed the oil." He turned the brown bottle upside down and poured some into his palm. "Watch in the mirror," he said.

At first she couldn't see anything. Standing behind her, he started on her shoulders. "I didn't want to get any in your hair," he explained, rubbing oil into her shoulders. The cinnamon scent swirled and tickled her nose. He worked his way down her back, skillfully massaging the muscles over and between her shoulder blades.

"This would feel better if I were on the bed."

"So eager for me?" he chuckled.

Surprise, she realized she was.

He oiled the spot just above her ass. "Just wait." His slippery fingers quickly slid over her most private entrance, and she gasped in shocked surprise. In the mirror she saw that her nipples were tautly erect.

"My God," she breathed.

"Stand still."

"I don't know if I can." She swallowed. "My knees . . ."

He stood behind her, closer now. She could feel his erection pressing against her ass through his silk shorts. The heat of it permeated the cloth.

He poured more oil into his palms and ran them over her

stomach. She looked in the mirror and saw that famished black-wolf look in his eye. He roughly massaged her breasts, pushing them together, making her seem much more voluptuous than she was. Watching his capable hands mold her breasts into such erotic positions, she couldn't believe it was her.

In the mirror, their gazes met. Both smoldered. He surrounded her. Everything she had, he could touch, suck, caress. And she wanted him to.

When his hand ran over the newly shaved area, Zoe moaned and dropped her head back against his shoulder. When his hand slid between her thighs and his talented fingertips slithered over her clit, she knew she'd do whatever he asked.

"No, not here. Get into bed."

She staggered toward it, and put her head on the pillow.

"Have you finally lost your need to control everything?" he whispered.

Incapable of speech, only a small sound came from the back of her throat. She ached for his touch. "I want you, Phillip."

"Remember," he said softly. "I give the orders." He straddled her and gathered her wrists. Somehow, he grabbed a silken cord, and he tied her hands to the headboard.

"I'll do whatever you want."

"Have you realized yet how liberating it is to have all choices made for you? I want your complete surrender, Zoe. I want all of you."

She lifted her wrists so he could more easily tie them.

He sat back and looked at her. A tantalizing finger traveled over her stomach and hip. "If you knew what you looked like—oiled, shaved, ready, willing . . ."

He ran his fingers over her pubic area, luxuriously letting the tips bump over her swollen clit. She groaned, "Please . . ." But not even she knew what she begged for.

Slowly, slowly, he traveled up to her breast. Feather light, he touched a nipple. As it hardened, he rolled it between his fingertips until she arched her back. It didn't take long. When he grabbed it between his teeth, she arched even more, begging him with her body to satisfy her.

With his mouth on her breast, he used his hand to nudge her thighs apart. She responded by opening them widely. How had she ever lived without this?

"Roll over on your belly."

She did, taking him with her. She heard his foot hit the nightstand clock and it tumbled to the floor.

"Zoe?"

"What—" she managed to gasp.

"The bet's over. It's past noon. You can do whatever you want." Phillip pulled the cords and freed her.

She sat up and wrapped her arms around him. As her slippery breast glided across his chest, he groaned. When he didn't stop her, she grabbed his lips in her own and kissed him as if her life depended on it.

"This is what I want," she gasped.

She ran her hand down his back and caught his bottom lip between her teeth. He grunted in agreement.

While caressing his chest with her breasts, she asked, "You know what that means?"

He ran his hands down her back and over her ass. "Don't leave." It was almost a plea.

"Do you want me to stay?"

"Yes."

"You know," she said, lifting a breast to his hungry mouth. "The 'no penetration' clause is now officially null and void."

He groaned and ran his fingers between her legs. As he slid inside, mere millimeters, she backed away and said, "Take off your shorts."

He did, and when her eyes landed on his cock, she saw desire in his eyes.

"It's nice to give an occasional order," she said.

He stood there as she flattened herself against the bed. She spread her legs to give him a glimpse of herself, teasing him. As she opened her mouth in anticipation for his broad purpled head, he groaned again. She took him in without hesitation.

The suction, the swirling—within moments he pulled her up. "Stop, please." His voice was hoarse. "Not like this." She tugged him with one more suck, and he pounced on her. Or maybe she pounced on him. She couldn't tell.

Between kisses, she heard him gasping her name. It did something to her. It melted her completely. While she'd been busy fighting her pride, he'd found a way to her heart.

He fumbled in the drawer for a condom and slid it on. She was wet and she was ready, but he didn't rush in. He pulled her so that she straddled him. His cock pulsated against her sex. He moved his mouth from hers, downward.

Knowing what he wanted, she pushed a breast to his mouth. She was so willing, so willing.

As he licked and sucked and bit at the stiff nipple, desire coiled in a tight ball in her belly. She twisted to present her other breast to his mouth, enjoying the shift in pressure of his cock against her clit. He obliged, hungrily, grazing his teeth against the other nipple and pressing harder against her.

"Now," she said, at the same time that he said, "Now."

"Yes," she moaned, pushing herself toward him. His hands encircled her tiny waist and pulled her fully on top of him. He thrust his hips upward in an invitation that she accepted. Ravenous, Zoe wrapped her legs more tightly around his hips, caught hold of his cock, and lifted herself just right. Tightening her thighs, she grabbed him and pulled until he sank into her, spreading her, filling her deliciously full. She shuddered.

She felt him shudder, too.

"God, Zoe . . ." Phillip pushed her onto her back, pushing

more deeply inside of her. She felt her muscles clamping onto him.

The magnitude of his desire for her filled her. Under him, she began to work, meeting each of his thrusts. She could hardly bear the pleasure of the penetration, and she hoped he was as close to ecstasy as she was.

Gasping, she couldn't look away from his face. She saw his jaw flex in an effort to control himself. Forced to keep her strokes short with his body on top of hers, she let his cock sink deliciously inside of her. Suddenly, she knew she was one nudge, one feather touch, away.

Phillip roared, "I need to . . . !"

She thrust herself up and he thrust down one more fulfilling drive.

"Phillip!" she cried, as the orgasm sizzled across her nerves in a delicious explosion.

Deep inside her, she could feel the pulsing of his thick cock.

Later, as they clung together in the sea of his bed, she ran her hand over his chest, thighs, wherever she could reach. The planes of his body fascinated her.

"Mmmmm. That was . . ." She couldn't think of anything good enough.

"Yeah," he agreed groggily.

"Having you inside of me felt great."

He whispered in her ear, "Do I have to keep winning bets to get you into bed?"

Just then, she knew she'd never be able to think of herself as the Ice Queen again. But where did that leave her at the firm? She just didn't want to think about that yet.

"Sorry," she said, teasingly. "We have to skip the second date."

"Why?" He sounded so horrified that she grinned.

"I really don't want to be spanked."

He ran his palm over her ass, caressing, promising. "You're all talk, Lauterborn. You don't even know yourself yet."

"You keep saying that," she said, as if she doubted him.

"Okay," Phillip said, relenting with a tired grin. "We'll save it for the third date."

"Bastard," she said, sweetly, getting up.

She walked around the bed and tripped over the clock. It read 11:45.

"You bastard." This time her tone was not sweet—not at all. "You lied to me."

"What?"

" 'No penetration' remember?"

"But you wanted it."

"I don't remember that as part of the terms."

"Zoe—"

"There's only one solution to this."

Phillip sat up, scratching his head, looking extremely displeased. "What's that?"

"Let's see if it's just as good after twelve." Zoe climbed back in bed.

9

"Hey, Lauterborn," Paul Thompson said. His tall, lanky frame filled the entrance to her new office. "You look different." At her expression, he laughed. "No, in a good way!"

"Can we lose this last-name thing?"

"Sure, boss," he said. "So? Did you get contacts?"

"Forget it," she said smiling. "Thanks for coming over. Have a seat."

"What's up?"

"We need someone to talk to the head of Freedom Mutual and soothe him. He needs a careful touch, but from a man."

"You want me to do it?" Paul asked doubtfully. "Adler's kind of . . ."

Zoe watched him search for a political word. "Prickly?" she suggested.

"Yeah, prickly."

"You think you can do it?"

"Maybe." Paul paused and said, "What do we know about him?"

"He's worried about rising interest rates, and he's right to be worried. The Feds keep threatening to up the rates. We need him to focus on the long term, quit watching the Fed chairman."

"Long term's our strength," Paul said, repeating the company mantra.

"Exactly! Can you get him to understand that? I mean without bullying him."

"It's hard not to push him," Paul mused. "He's so stubborn."

"You're young and hip. Make him feel cool." Zoe looked at the ceiling for a minute then said, "You've got to make him think it's his idea. Make him think he was always focused on long-term payoffs."

"I can do that," he said, with growing assurance.

"I think so, too."

"Thanks." Paul looked pleased at her vote of confidence.

"Can you call him at three?"

"Sure. I'll let you know how it goes." Paul stood to leave. "Oh," he said. "Marci and I are going to Lucky Chan's tonight. You want to come with us?"

"Sounds like fun." Marci worked in accounting, and her dry sense of humor appealed to Zoe. Marci and Paul were becoming something of a couple. "But I've got plans tonight."

"Hot date, huh?"

"Maybe," she said, playfully.

"Bring him along. The more the merrier."

"He's got something special planned, he says."

"Phillip's a lucky guy." Paul started to walk away.

"Hey, Paul?"

"Yeah?"

"It's not contacts. I'm wearing my hair down."

Zoe checked her clock and stood. She had just enough time for a lipstick check before the next meeting. His husky voice stopped her in her tracks.

"I'd love to be that tiny strap around your ankle." His voice was so low only she could hear him. "I'd find a way to slither up—"

"Phillip, how do you handle a single fund?" she teased. "You're always thinking about—"

"You." The deep affection in his voice sent a shiver down her spine.

She refrained from caressing his neck, barely.

"What'd you do to make Paul so happy?" Phillip asked.

"Is he happy?"

"He was singing his way down the hallway."

Zoe laughed. "I'm lucky to have him on the team. I gave him a difficult job that I knew he could do.

"Brilliant." He grinned, suggestively. "Think you could handle me that well?"

"I've done a pretty good job so far," she said lightly.

"I think so, too."

Zoe smiled and walked away. Over her shoulder she said, "Go manage something, Phillip."

"Congratulations," said Phillip, as they strolled around the Washington Square Park fountain. "You're an amazing boss." His honest pleasure made her heart expand, filling her chest. She knew a weaker man would have been jealous.

"Thanks."

"Partnerships are becoming second nature for you."

Something in his tone grabbed her attention.

"This is it." Phillip pointed toward the bench they'd used on that spring night.

"Oh," said Zoe. A streak of heat raced through—the passion of his touch always did that to her.

"You didn't mind losing that bet so much," Phillip reminded her, tugging her next to him on the bench. He enveloped her hand in both of his. She savored the warmth of it.

At the end of the day, she *hadn't* minded losing. "No," she agreed. "I like who I am with you. I like us together."

"I love you, Zoe." He pulled her into his arms and held her a moment without speaking. She inhaled deeply, loving the masculine scent of him, the safety of his embrace. "Do I have to ask your father first?" Could she hear a smile in his voice?

"You can ask, but he'll just laugh. He knows it's up to me—to us." Her heart was pounding double-time now.

"In that case . . ." Phillip slid from the bench and on to one knee.

"Oh," Zoe said, her eyes widening with growing joy.

He cleared his throat. "Zoe Lynn," Phillip said, pulling a small box from his pocket.

Tiffany's trademark blue bow caught her attention, and the magnitude of the moment made her heart nearly stop. She wanted to capture this feeling forever in her memory. Zoe looked away, seeing a sliver of sinking sun between a forest of skyscrapers. She couldn't look away from the light.

Phillip opened the box and handed it to her. "Will you marry me?"

SLOW HAND

BONNIE EDWARDS

*For Barb Briggs and Judy Jackson, dear friends and co-queens.
And for Ted, the man of my dreams.*

1

Jared MacKay crossed his bare feet on the top railing of the *SandJack* and slid his cap down to cover his face. He deserved this nap, worked hard for this nap. He wanted this nap more than anything else he could think of.

But the unmistakable thrum of wheeled luggage on the dock intruded. He told himself to ignore it, to focus instead on the icy bottle between his fingers as it drizzled cold droplets of condensation onto his belly. A chilly brew in his hand, the sun hot on his skin and the sound of the Caribbean lapping against the hull were all he needed to coax himself into sleep.

He let everything go and prepared to settle in but the staccato tap of high heels joined the low rumble from the dock. He gave in to his curiosity, tilted his cap back just enough to look. He kept his eyes slitted against the sun and watched the sure advance of a seductive piece of woman.

Minus the stilettos she'd be all of five-foot-two. Blond, good legs, athletic body.

Tightly wound, tightly focused, tightly built.

Her suitcase snagged on a rope Jean-Paul, his neighbor, had left strewn across the dock, and she turned to lift the wheels.

Her ass, encased in a short white skirt, was as prime as the rest of her. Taut, high and lush, her cheeks made a man think of molding her, opening her and sliding into tight, hot places.

Bad, bad timing, MacKay. The luggage train told him she was most likely the bride half of his next charter clients. If this was his reaction now, heaven help him when he heard her cry out in passion.

Passion he had no hand in. Shit.

The *SandJack* was a solidly built thirty-five footer, but sometimes it was all he could do to ignore what happened below-decks, especially with a screamer.

And this petite blond hottie looked like a screamer. He slid the bottle to his lap to cover his rod which had come to life at first sight of her. She'd gotten past Jean-Paul's rope now and was headed his way again.

So much for his nap. Even if he did manage to catch one, it would be all about dreams anyway. Hot dreams. Scorching dreams. Nails-down-his-back dreams. He shifted his focus back to her.

Her eyes were shielded by wraparound sunglasses, but nothing could hide the exquisite bounce of breasts under the silky tank top she wore.

To keep himself in check, he looked past her, needing to see the man she had in tow. The guy would reek of money and success and would never know how the sight of his bride had kick-started a lust as big as the *SandJack* herself. But there was no man following her, no man at the top of the pier paying off a cab, no man anywhere.

He swung his gaze back to the grim set of her lips, the wilted curl in her hair, the definite lack of makeup. Flustered, hot and disheveled, she didn't look the way the brides usually did. She looked . . . angry.

When they'd spoken on the phone, her voice had been harried and demanding. He'd put it down to standard wedding nerves but now, seeing her rigid stride, he wasn't so sure. There were people who were always imperious and he didn't do well with imperious. Not well at all.

He'd keep that in mind for the next few days while he did his best to ignore her. He sure as hell didn't want this itch all week, not if she continued to look so sour. He slid his cap back down to cover his face and waited for her to park herself and her luggage alongside. It wouldn't do to look too interested. There was no telling when her man would show up. He didn't want to be caught leering at the bride with a woody the size of a bowsprit.

"Mr. MacKay?" Teri Branton asked, pleased at how clear her voice sounded. No one would know from her voice how vicious her day had been.

The man on the *SandJack* twitched as if she'd woken him. She probably had. He had the insolent look of a man used to doing a lot of nothing. His feet were propped against the railing, giving her a worm's eye view up the back side of his khaki shorts. Strong lean legs, tanned beyond healthy, big bare feet with strong toes and callused soles.

He slid his ball cap to the back of his head, revealing a powerful face. Powerful because his lean nose and slashing thin lips were too cutting to be handsome. But they held her attention just the same. Then he opened his eyes and focused on her.

Cut by the laser blue that stared back at her, Teri's heart fluttered at the intensity and she took a single step back. Tired of being intimidated, she caught herself before taking another.

"You *are* the captain of the *SandJack*?" she asked.

"Take off your shoes." His voice had a deep timbre that stroked her insides from breastbone to toes, so she wasn't sure what she'd heard.

"Excuse me?"

"Those shoes," he tilted his chin down to indicate her feet. "Take them off."

A fierce light from his gaze burned into hers as he waited.

And then she knew. He wasn't the captain of this vessel. He was a pirate, a rogue, a brigand. He was danger. And excitement.

A thrill chased down her belly.

She looked at her feet and saw incongruous white satin stilettos with a delicate spray of seed pearls trailing the outside edge.

Her wedding shoes.

She was still in them.

Odd that she'd forgotten to change. When she'd found them after a hunt through every store in Manhattan, a perfect fit, she'd paid a fortune for them. They'd meant a lot to her at the time. Now, they just looked . . . sad.

Stepping wide, she saw the pirate follow her movement, then track the shape of her legs up from her feet to her knees and higher.

Interesting.

He was checking her out! Awareness of her own power gripped her as she numbly regarded her shoes, and thought about the pirate's interest.

The intensity she'd given to the hunt for these perfect shoes was gone as surely as smoke in the wind. With as much substance. Stupid how her wedding had taken over her life, her every waking moment. Her back felt tired from these shoes, her toes ached from every pair of stilettos she owned. The fatigue seeped from her pinched toes, up her calves and into her lower spine.

She wanted to sag with the weight of her day, but then in her peripheral vision, she saw the pirate move his beer to his lips. He took a sip from the bottle, waiting with obvious patience for her to do whatever it was she was planning to do with the shoes.

She looked at him again, saw the hot blue of his eyes, the long lean length of his legs, the strength in his hands. Then she considered the very private week ahead of her.

She'd decided to spend the time eating too much, drinking too much and mulling her life. But now, this pirate presented another opportunity. An exciting opportunity for overindulgence of a different kind.

Besides, she was sick of men giving her orders and making demands, from her ex-fiancé, to a whole TV production crew. And this man looked arrogant as hell, supremely confident and in need of lessons in polite conversation.

Slanting him a glance, she realized she was in just the right mood to give this *captain* the lessons he needed.

Aware that he watched her, she bent down, slowly slid her right shoe off. With a surreptitious glance, she saw his gaze sharpen to intense focus. She set the shoe on the dock. Definitely had his attention now.

She bent over again, gave her ass an extra tilt and ran her hand down her left leg to her ankle, grasped the back of her left shoe and slid it off too. He still watched, his eyes hooded with the pretense of nonchalance, but she knew better.

She set her left shoe beside her right on the dock, in perfect alignment. The seed pearls glowed with the warm sheen nature had given them.

But somehow it wasn't enough to remove the shoes. It wasn't enough to have him look at her toes as she wiggled them, nails painted pink and pearly in the sunshine. No, this little display wasn't nearly enough to satisfy her.

She lifted each shoe, balanced them on her open palms, and tilted first one then the other into the brine. They landed on their sides and began to fill with water.

A lightness filled her at their silent drowning. She smiled as they sank.

The pirate dropped his feet to the deck, stood and leaned over the rail to see them go.

One floated a couple seconds longer than the other, but in the end, they drifted to the bottom, lost. "You didn't have to pitch them."

"Yes, I did."

He looked at her with a question in his eyes. "Jared MacKay, captain of the *SandJack*, at your service."

"Teri Branton," she responded.

He looked up the dock toward the street. "Where's the groom?"

"Missing in action."

He looked perplexed. "He's not aboard. Did you lose him on the way from the airport?"

"No."

His eyebrow quirked with an unspoken question.

Teri ignored it because she hadn't yet considered what to say when people asked. She held out her hand for help to climb over the railing to the deck.

He obliged. A snap of electricity arced between them at first touch. She dropped his hand immediately. The burn in her palm made her smooth her smarting hand across her skirt.

He stared at his hand as if he'd been stung. "Feel that?"

Down to her toes. "Yes. We'll try again."

"No! No way. I'm not touching you again." The shocked vehemence in his tone appalled her.

"How am I supposed to get over the railing?"

"Here." He leaned over the side and dropped a step stool onto the dock. "Use this."

"Yes, sir," she snapped, hiking her skirt so she could lift her leg over. She teetered midstraddle and had to stretch out her arm for balance. He made a grab for her waist, then dropped her to the deck like a sack of potatoes and jumped back.

The tang of his touch reverberated through her ribcage and settled like fire around her heart. Must be the airline food. She patted her chest. "Heartburn."

"Sure, yeah, that's what it is." But he was running his other hand up and down the arm he'd wrapped around her. He frowned like thunder and vaulted over the railing. Next, he hefted her suitcases to the boat in a smoothly athletic maneuver that belied his earlier lethargy.

Teri stood back and admired Jared MacKay's superb body. He was well toned and muscular without bulk. His thick black hair curled around his ears and the wicked slash of his hard mouth sent a thrill from her chest to the soles of her feet.

Oh my.

She was going to sea with this man. For seven days and six nights.

One week. Adrift. Alone.

Six months of celibacy caught up to her and a long dead heaviness reawakened in her lowest belly.

A sensible woman would go to a hotel and lick her wounds in private. But *sensible* was not what she wanted, not after today.

Right now, she wanted this adventure. She wanted, probably needed, she realized in a clear moment of self-preservation, the delicious naughtiness of being alone with a stranger who got her hot at first sight. She wanted him, Jared MacKay. And she wanted him bad. Very bad.

She shifted, letting her upper thighs touch and rub. The heartburn dived to her loins where it set a candle to burn.

He stood for a long moment looking hopefully along the dock toward the street.

"Waiting for someone?" she asked.

"The groom."

"If he did show up, I'd push him overboard." She liked the idea of Philip nibbled to a slow death by sea creatures. "The groom isn't coming."

He glanced at her, but turned back to his study of the pier. "Really," she added and then thought about what she'd said. "Well, he's not coming with me. It's been at least six months since he did that."

The pirate swung to her, eyes shocked wide.

"I'm here for my honeymoon alone."

2

There, it was out, she'd said it. There was no groom. Teri tilted her chin up, refused to feel anything but angry and maybe a touch grateful, although that was a surprising response she'd think about later.

The captain's shock turned to heat as he accepted what she'd said. He too, understood the possibilities between them for the week. A sudden shift in his gaze gave her a strange and confusing thought. Was he afraid of her? She dismissed the crazy idea as soon as it popped into her head.

"Stay right here. Don't move," he instructed. He headed down a narrow flight of stairs that led below. He was a full head and shoulders taller than she and must outweigh her by forty pounds. What would he have to fear from her?

Ignoring his instructions, she followed him to the head of the stairs and peeked down to see what he was up to.

Jared MacKay was stripping down a honeymoon congratulations banner, replacing wine flutes with tumblers and removing an ice bucket and champagne bottle from beside the bed.

He was de-honeymooning the *SandJack*.

A pirate with heart. Who'd have thought she'd stumble onto such a man when she felt this heartsore?

Not heartbroken, she realized with a start, just sore. She rubbed her hand over her heart. It beat strong and true, even a little rapidly, at the thought of her honeymoon for one turning into something for two.

Jared whisked a package into the medicine chest she could just see from her vantage point. Then he slid some DVDS into a drawer by the bed.

He gave her the all clear and she took down one small overnight bag to unpack. He carried the rest of the bigger suit-cases below, careful not to touch her again when he handed them off to her. Without a word he headed back up to take the *SandJack* out of Kingston harbor.

Shit! Jared's mind spun and his arm still burned where he'd held Teri to lift her over the rail. He should turn around and dump her back on the pier and escape while he could. He rubbed his chest and swiped a hand across the back of his neck. He was sweating.

Shit!

His palm still held the memory of the sting he'd felt at their first touch. He rubbed his palm across his thigh, but found no relief. Like a bee sting, it throbbed, reminding him, making him think crazy thoughts.

His father's and more recently his brother's words echoed.

"It's hot. Snaps like a brand you can never remove. A couple more touches, you won't want to remove it." He envisioned the grins on their faces, the red that'd seeped up to their ears. Saps, both of them.

Wrong, too.

Love was not a firebrand. Did not scorch the skin. Did not appear out of nowhere. Did *not* come at first touch.

Love grew slowly. Over time. With the right woman. When

a man was ready. He'd lived by that mantra his whole life. Had based his marriage on the idea.

The other two males in the MacKay family had scoffed when he'd married Gina. He'd pretty much cut them out of his life for the next six months, but eventually, he'd eaten crow. The marriage died a slow gentle death.

Teri Branton wanted a week at sea. She was here for a honeymoon that wasn't. The display she'd put on for him with those shoes had let him know she was looking for action.

Revenge sex? Maybe. If so, he'd be happy to take her up on it, in spite of the live wire that snapped and bit whenever they touched. He'd adjust because there was no way in hell he was going to let a chance at a woman like that go by just because his brother and father were crazy. No way.

For now he focused on navigating Kingston harbor, avoiding smaller and larger craft. He waved to other charter boats heading in for the night and wished like hell he'd never thought up this honeymoon charter idea. Day trips paid well enough and all he'd have to do was promise snacks and drinks.

But no, he hadn't been satisfied with a casual income, had to go after the guarantee of advance bookings. Had to turn this easygoing venture into a full-time career. When he'd decided to go for it, he'd been happy to get back into the game.

His time for drifting had come to an end.

And who has to show up? A woman who shoots sparks.
Shit!

Alone below, Teri took in how sumptuous the boat was. The Web site hadn't done it justice. Pleased, she noted an extra-long cream-colored leather sofa along one side. A couple of armchairs completed the furnishings while a plasma screen television was set on the wall. Light wood cabinets kept the cooking area from being dark. She marveled at the ingenious use of space and opened every cupboard she saw.

The bathroom off the master cabin was small but well appointed with a shower set in a tiny tub. She opened the medicine chest over the sink to check out what it was that Jared had put away. A variety pack of condoms: glow in the dark, flavored and ribbed for her pleasure.

Extra large.

She snorted. Philip should be so lucky.

Back in the master cabin she checked out the drawer in the night table. The DVDs Jared had put away were X-rated. She popped one into the player, propped herself on the bed and skipped through the beginning to find couples enjoying strong, healthy, powerful sex. Great sex. Friendly sex. Even affectionate sex.

Philip's pious expression when he'd explained the concept of revirginizing swam in front of her mind's screen. He wanted them to remember their wedding night as special, he'd said. She'd been amazingly agreeable. It had been so easy to give up sleeping with him, she should have seen the signs of a dying relationship.

But by then the wedding had taken on a life of its own, a juggernaut, there was no stopping it. His mother, her mother, the caterer, the church, the dress!

None of the energetic sex she saw on the portable bedroom television had ever happened with Philip. She sighed, wandered out to the little kitchen, retrieved the champagne from the fridge, opened it and poured herself a tumbler full. She considered digging out the flutes Jared had put away but the tumbler held more. And Teri wanted lots.

When she settled back onto the bed a couple onscreen were enjoying a fabulously decadent soixante-neuf. The actor's tongue work looked enthusiastic. The actress looked happy.

Teri watched closely, amused at first. The moaning and sex talk were obviously dubbed in afterward. No one really said things like that, no one felt things as strongly as the actors pretended.

She changed positions on the bed, lying on her belly with her head at the foot so she could see the action up close. And up close was what she got.

The camera closed in on his tongue so Teri could see the moisture, the red, full clit he was licking and sucking gently between his lips.

Her own body reacted to the visual stimulus and moistened as the actress widened her legs and the actor slid his tongue deep into her. She thrashed on the bed in a stunning display of sexual hysteria that had never, ever overcome Teri.

She was jealous. Did people react this strongly to oral sex? She never had. But, then, Philip was so fastidious she doubted he'd ever been as deeply involved as the actor was. Even an actor who was being paid to fake it was more turned on than Philip had been the few times she'd insisted.

Teri knew what she wanted, knew what she liked, knew what would get her off like a rocket, but Philip had issues.

She'd always hoped he'd warm up more. Get hotter, get horny. For her. But he hadn't. Wouldn't. Not ever.

The onscreen couple switched positions and the actress performed fellatio until the man bucked and howled with his orgasm. The couple tumbled onto the sofa, sated.

Teri clicked off the TV, took another long drink and rolled onto her back. Her legs slid open and she felt herself, moist and heavy with need.

The bedroom door was open and from the bed she could see through the living area and up the stairs to one small rectangular patch of sky. She wondered what would happen if Jared were to peer down the hatch and see her here with her legs splayed and her hand on her wet slit.

Would the pirate on deck come down to the master cabin

and grab her ankles like the actor had? She closed her eyes and let her fantasy play out. It was better than any porn flick because she could control every movement, every word and all of her responses. She could tell Jared what to do and he'd do it.

She could tell him to lick her breasts and lift her hips to bring her closer to his mouth. He could trail his scratchy chin delicately along her inner thigh until he got close enough that she could feel his hot breath on her hotter pussy. She slid her other hand to a nipple and plucked it while she opened to her questing fingertip.

She would tell him to linger there, just far enough away from her that he'd be able to see her wet lips, smell her aroused flesh, feel her need. Sliding a fingertip into herself, familiar tension built while she worked to bring herself to orgasm. He would kiss her there where she was hottest, moist and achy. He'd do whatever she told him to and like it.

She wasn't wired for abstinence, hadn't wanted to go along with Philip's crazy idea, but—oh, yes, it was building to a peak now and soon she'd be over the—on a weak sigh, her orgasm pulsed through her lower body in a poor imitation of what she'd witnessed onscreen.

She opened her eyes on the wish that Jared had seen her, that he was right now on his way to ravish her like the pirate he was. But no, he'd been a gentleman and left her to herself.

Her unsatisfied self.

She'd taken the edge off, but it had been far too long since she'd had a truly good orgasm. And she deserved one. Or three.

Or a week full of them. She smiled and rose to wash her hands. In the mirror, she faced herself.

Philip was gone. She was here. Jared was here.

And Jared was hot, hot, hot.

She decided to unpack her lingerie after all.

Her carry-on bag sat on the floor beside the bed, tagged and zipped and bulging. A couple of sharp points threatened to poke holes through the sides, but still, she couldn't bring herself to open it.

She took another drink of champagne instead.

The bag was full of shoes. Stilettos, each and every pair. Toes pointed enough to cripple, Philip always wanted her to wear them. If he'd wanted a tall, lanky, long-limbed wife why had he asked her out in the first place? She would never have that look, no matter how high her heels were. She was lean, yes, but her muscle tone was obvious.

Some men liked her athletic build. The pirate above decks for one, she realized as she poured and drank another tumbler of champagne. She sat on the edge of the bed, one toe on the floor for balance, the other heel tucked into her crotch. She bent over toward the night table to grab the bottle again, but nearly fell off the bed.

She was tipsy. Well and truly feeling no pain. She giggled.

Oh, hell, who cared? There was no one here to judge her. No one to tell her she'd had too much and had to mind herself.

No one to tell her to keep her hands to herself and off Jared MacKay.

"Step away from the pirate," she intoned in a dramatic imitation of Philip's most commanding tone. Then she laughed harder.

Philip had no say in anything she did anymore. He'd given up the right to chastise her, instruct her or humiliate her when he'd dashed out of the church this morning.

She stood, still laughing, curiously aware of an incredible sense of freedom. She set aside her carry-on bag. She'd open it later. Right now she wanted her bathing suit and sarong.

There was a sunset waiting for her.

A sunset and a pirate who needed taming.

3

Teri reappeared on deck after they left harbor, dressed in a thong bikini with a see-through gauzy white skirt that fell to her ankles.

She hung like a wraith in Jared's peripheral vision as he steered clear of other boats and watched the water for obstacles.

She wandered up to the bow, book in hand. What kind of man wouldn't care that his bride brought a book on her honeymoon?

What kind of man would let a woman like this get away?

He knew when she sat on a deck chair. He knew when she opened her paperback, caught at an errant tendril of hair, opened her skirt to get some failing sunlight on her legs. Toned legs, shapely legs that ended on pearly pink toes.

He liked pink so much better than red. Red painted nails just said come and get it. Pink made a man wonder how hot she could get.

The breeze blew her hair back from her face. The wind put color in her cheeks and he just knew her lips were moist and soft and pouty. Perfect lips, perfect teeth and a perfect pink tongue to lick him with.

His hands clamped hard on the wheel, but his gaze slid down from her face to her chest, where hard pebbles pushed out of the little triangles that covered the tips of her breasts. The wind had blown the skirt between her thighs, outlining her. From here, he could see the line of her white thong bikini bottom as it disappeared between her legs. He clamped the wheel harder and remembered the threat of the snap and crackle on his hand and arm, reminding him not to touch her again.

He still hadn't seen her eyes. She'd kept her sunglasses on the whole time. Were they green? Blue? Soft? Hard? Did they telegraph her thoughts or was she adept at hiding them?

He bet on her being wide open. Otherwise she wouldn't need to hide behind the glasses, she'd have taken them off earlier.

He studied the shoulder length, blond hair and decided she was born with it. A sleek cigarette boat appeared on the starboard side. The sailors waved and the speedboat crossed his bow well ahead of the *SandJack*.

Teri waved back and laughed at the smaller boat then put her bare feet up on the railing the same way he had earlier.

Now she was going to take the nap he'd wanted.

She slid down in the chair so she could stretch far enough to set her feet more squarely on the rail. The movement caused the skirt to fall clear of her legs, exposing them. Great legs.

"You'll burn," he called. "Either cover up or use the sunscreen under the chair."

She tilted her face toward him. "Sunburn even in this light?"

"You're pale and fair. This is Jamaican sun. Better to be safe."

She felt around under her seat and came up with a bottle. She popped the top, held the container high over her other hand and squeezed. A slow white stream of lotion drizzled into her palm.

His mouth went dry as she lifted her left leg and began long slow strokes to apply it. She started at her toes and worked up to her ankle, swirling the creamy stuff around to the heel and back to the front. Her pink painted fingernails trailed up to her calves and rubbed the lotion into her skin.

He hung on every smooth satiny movement of flesh as she kneaded and slathered and poured more from the bottle. Behind her knee where heat pooled, up her thighs, inside and outside. She stood, let the gauzy skirt drop to the teak deck and rubbed her hand across her left ass cheek. Creaming more lotion into her hand, she went back to a thorough covering of her high taut buttock.

Sweat broke out on his forehead. His T-shirt was long since damp. His shorts strained until he made an adjustment.

He'd seen lots of women apply sunscreen. Been invited to join the game countless times. Had smoothed his share of fine asses, but this, this was like something out of a teenage boy's dream.

The last thought he had before all control settled south of his waistband, was that he didn't give a damn about static charges or electricity or even fate. After that, his other head was in charge.

"Need help?" The pirate's voice sounded strained and Teri smiled to herself.

"Not with this," she called back.

The champagne had gone to her head, the movie she'd seen had aroused her, while her weak little orgasm had only served to remind her of how much more she needed.

As much as she wanted to let all those things dictate her behavior, her sensible side told her to slow down, take it easy, she'd been through too much to process in a few short hours. She shouldn't add the seduction of a perfect stranger to the mix.

Perfect. That was the operative word here, her other, definitely dangerous side said. Jared MacKay was the perfect stranger. Sexy, hot, available.

No one, but no one need ever know about what went on between them.

Just the idea excited her.

Her hand filled with lotion and reminded her of what she was doing. Getting back into the game of seduction, she repositioned her chair with one hand so that she was sideways to Jared at the wheel. She took her seat again and slathered the lotion all over her right leg.

When she reached the top of her thigh, she allowed her fingertip to slide under the G-string that separated her folds between her legs. She rubbed lotion under the *vee* of material that covered her mons pubis.

Slicking the lotion around her lowest belly she made sure he saw her tilt her head back in a parody of sexual yearning. She jutted her hips up toward her hand miming the act of self gratification.

The idea that he watched from the wheel as she played at pleasuring herself excited her. She made bets on how long it would take before he succumbed to the need that wafted around her, pulsing like a force of nature.

Peeping at him from lowered lids, it thrilled her to see him completely focused on her. Intent and narrow, his gaze tracked every slide of her fingertip. The muscles in his forearms stood out as he gripped the wheel tight and hard.

The pirate was turned on. An erection jutted under his shorts and made her mouth water. It had been far too long since she'd swirled her tongue across the head of an erect penis. She wondered about his scent and how he tasted, how much leakage he had when he was ready to explode. Oh, how she loved the taste of the slick stuff that hinted at the wealth of semen he carried.

Her eyes slid closed as moisture built between her legs. Her finger slid a millimeter lower and she felt the tip of her protruding clitoris. One delicate brush was all she needed to bring another slide of moisture to her inner lips. If she wasn't careful, she really would be pleasuring herself again and she already knew that wasn't enough to ease the ache she felt.

She removed her finger from under her thong and stood, pulling her sarong skirt up to cover herself again.

She tied it at her waist and leaned over the railing to watch the bow slice through the water. Placing her feet wide apart on the deck, she let the vibration from the engine seep into her soles, up her legs to massage her heart.

The wind kicked up the ends of her hair and she raised her arms out from her sides, turning them into wings. How she wanted to fly, to lift away from this churning upheaval and soar away on an updraft that would take her far away.

Oblivion, that's what she wanted. She could drink herself into it, eat chocolate until she exploded or have wild sex with a pirate all week.

She settled her chin on her hand. The drinking would make her feel sick, the chocolate would settle on her hips and the sex, well, she couldn't see much of a downside. The actors she'd watched earlier had certainly enjoyed themselves.

She thought about that. Sex with an audience might be fun. Sex with a bunch of people standing around with lights, cameras and instructions for louder moans, more sweat, better orgasms might make her wild, bring out her inner sex kitten.

Her mind swirled, kicked up a series of images from the movie that excited her. She easily overlaid Jared's face with the actor she'd seen. She became the actress making such spectacular use of Jared's tongue. But it wasn't the movie or her fantasy that excited her, it was the pirate. The pirate and the promise she saw in his gaze.

Hot promise.

"Don't lean too far over," he called. "Go overboard there and you're lost for sure."

She turned to face him. He was standing at the wheel. The wind caught at the curls at the nape of his neck, the sun kissed his shoulders and strong forearms. Her mouth watered.

She set her elbows on the railing and crossed her ankles, content for the moment to let her gaze wander around the boat.

The *SandJack* boasted a hot tub on deck, several lounge chairs and heavily padded bunks along the edges. The deck itself was wooden and she guessed her heels would have left gouges.

She wriggled her toes against the deck. She hadn't been barefoot in years. She missed it.

The bone-deep heat from the sun eased away her tension and she grinned at the way her most disastrous day ever had turned out. No matter what Philip was doing, she was having the time of her life.

No phones, no e-mail, no mother-in-law, no arrangements to make, no faking smiles when she felt like screaming.

Just sun, waves and a man she wanted to ravish.

What more could a jilted bride ask for?

4

Jared focused on the woman leaning with her back to the bow. She was watching him as closely as he watched her. The show she'd put on with the lotion had him iron hard, and if it weren't for the words of warning in his head, he'd have been on her faster than a shark on bait.

Static, that's all it had been. Hell, he'd felt sharper jolts crossing a carpet and touching a television. His father and brother were crazy wrong.

Women didn't spark like live wires and take a man down. They just didn't. And even if there was a woman out there who was going to grab his heart and not let go it wouldn't be this one.

He'd already had an edgy, tightly wound spitfire in his life and he sure as hell didn't want another one. Too much maintenance. Too demanding. Too much energy.

But, Teri was hot and made it plain she knew what she wanted. Another plus was that she was a tourist with a life to go back to. A different life than she'd expected, but if she was the live wire he thought she was, she'd be antsy to get back on track with her career. A runaway groom would only be a minor setback.

Hot sex with a woman who knew what she wanted and how was a helluva temptation, in spite of his crazy brother and father.

So, to do her or not to do her? That was the question.

She turned sideways, giving him her profile, and caught her hair at the back of her head to hold it back. His heart stalled in his chest.

She was perfect. Round where he wanted round, full where he wanted full and smiling at him as if she knew it.

"Want dinner?" he asked because it was time to let her know he wouldn't be teased into responding too soon. No, the whole week would be better for them both if she knew who was in charge right from the start.

He was the captain, after all. Sparks be damned.

"Yes! I'm starving," she spoke as if surprised, and palmed her perfect belly.

He cut the throttle and slowed to a stop. The engine cut out, while the boat rocked on small swells. This was the first quiet bay out of Kingston, a spot where he normally served dinner. So far, the trip was right on schedule.

The smile on her face, the heat in her gaze and his rock-hard cock told him this would be the last time anything happened according to schedule.

He anchored and headed down to the galley.

She followed and sat on a bar stool to watch. "I'd help but it's so small I'd just get in the way."

"You're the client; besides, everything's ready to be heated and I'm used to doing this alone." He turned and opened the fridge, mentally tallying everything he needed.

"Do you cook all the meals?"

"I have a chef from one of the hotels cater for me. It was the last detail I had to arrange before starting up." He lifted the container of duck out of the fridge and turned to face her.

"They're blue," he said, startled by the simple beauty of her face without the sunglasses. For a moment he forgot he was holding the roasting pan and stared. "Really blue, like flowers, or . . . something."

She smiled and stared right back at him. "My eyes? Yes, they're blue." She looked down at the countertop. Tapped her fingers in a nervous tattoo. "Look, Jared, when I called to book the week I was brusque with you. I'm sorry. Things were pretty hectic at that point." She frowned. "Are you sure you don't want any help?"

"I'm not a natural cook, but I've got it covered." He slit the cover on the pan the way the chef had shown him. "Weddings make people cranky."

She looked thoughtful.

"Seems simple enough," he said. "Two people ready to pro-mise the rest of their lives to each other, a minister willing to hear them and some family and friends to celebrate afterward. But things are never that easy."

"You can say that again. My mother's a tank when she gets going and his mother's a perfectionist of the highest degree. It was a disaster waiting to happen."

"Have you spoken to him?"

"No."

He decided against using the fine china. They'd picnic on deck instead. "Alfresco all right?"

"Perfect." She set her chin in her hand, blew out a breath that made her breasts rise and fall. And her nipples looked like pearls tucked into her top.

He looked away, opened the microwave and slid the duck inside. "A lot of men would feel squeezed under those circum-stances. Was he refereeing, got fed up?"

"No, I played referee. It wasn't the stress of the wedding plans. Hell, the only thing I asked him to do was call you and he refused. But he made sure I had his list of demands."

Jared didn't know what to say.

"So, no, it wasn't the wedding itself. It was the affair he'd been having with my maid of honor."

"What?" He stopped midpoint between setting the power level and the time on the microwave control panel.

She tilted her chin up, a gesture he was beginning to understand was defensive.

"He listened to my vows. He watched my face the way most grooms do, then he looked over my shoulder at June. The silence went on and on while I waited. When it seemed like everyone was on the edge of their seats straining to hear the first word, he let go of my hand, reached for June's, and they raced back down the aisle out the church door."

The last was said all in a rush. He opened his mouth but he couldn't think of a damn thing that would take the edge off. "I'm trying like hell to think of something to say, but I've got nothing."

The corner of her mouth tilted upward. "Thanks for trying, but there's nothing *to* say. The church erupted into this weird kind of chatter and noise and the minister had to hold me up until my dad got to me. My mother was crying, his mother looked like she'd swallowed vinegar and his sister stood there smirking."

"And now?" he asked.

"Now I'm here to eat, drink and be merry. Want to help me be merry?"

He looked at her and she looked back, her sultry gaze drawing him in. He zeroed in on her mouth. She licked her bottom lip, leaving it moist. He saw her teeth, even and white and ready to nip at him. Christ, he was losing it over a glance! "I'm here to please," he said.

"Good. You can pour me more champagne."

"Happy to."

She held up her flute for a toast. "To us, the week and all the merrymaking the *SandJack* can provide."

He nodded. "We'll do our best."

"I'm sure you will."

She coaxed him into sharing some champagne. She didn't have to try very hard—he was more than ready to let go of his final reservations about having her.

"I'm glad you decided to come on your own," he said, angry enough at her story that he wanted to punch the guy's lights out.

She smiled in a mysterious way. "Well, I won't be doing that again for a while."

The air between them crackled and shrank, closing them into their game of hide and seek and advance and retreat. The *SandJack* never seemed so small, so tight, so in tune with the hot thoughts they each seemed to have.

The microwave chimed that the meal was ready and they carried everything they needed topside and settled on a blanket on deck. Jared still kept his distance, using the plates as buffers between their hands.

The *SandJack* rocked gently, the stars came out and Teri sat across from him propped against the railing, one foot raised to rest on the cooler of beer he'd brought onboard. He hadn't opened the ice-filled chest because it was full of a specific brand of beer her ex had requested.

The wind still played with her skirts and with her leg raised he got a better view of the dark mystery that hid behind the small triangle of material between her legs.

She knew he was looking, knew he wanted her, made it clear she wanted him, too.

The champagne continued to flow and as her words slurred and thoughts got fuzzy, he decided to back off. She didn't need a drunken lay on the deck. She needed some TLC, which was exactly what she'd get.

Besides, when he had her, he wanted her awake, aware and as hot for him as he was for her. The first time had to be one to remember, because he knew he always would.

When Jared headed below, Teri blew out a breath, sucked in another one and tried to sober up. If she didn't, she'd blow it for sure.

But then she got a watery image of Philip's smirking sister and poured herself another glass of champagne. The air had turned early evening calm, so quiet she was able to still her mind to think.

She'd been jilted, sure. Left at the altar, mouth agape as her fiancé ran out the door. But, right now, right here, with the breeze settling to a caress and the stars handing her a spectacular display, she wasn't as devastated as she ought to be. In fact, she enjoyed the growing sense of relief.

Of freedom.

Of awareness.

It had been six long months. A hell of a dry spell for an engaged woman and Jared MacKay was hot.

When she'd seen him with his long legs up on the deck railing she'd been surprised at how sexy he was. On the phone, when she'd been so frantic to make all the arrangements Philip had demanded, Jared sounded bored and disinterested. She'd wondered if he would show much enthusiasm for taking care of them for these few days.

But now, she suspected he'd been having an off day, because the way he looked at her was anything but bored. Intense and aware, Jared knew what she wanted and was ready to give it to her. It was just a matter of how long they could play the game before they jumped each other. The anticipation made Teri smile and made her even more deliciously aware of the heat between her legs. She shifted and squeezed the tops of her thighs together, feeling herself moisten at the friction. She'd caught him glancing at her there, and knew he'd enjoyed the game she'd played with the sunblock.

Jared returned with a couple of light cotton pullovers. He held one out to her.

"I didn't think you'd want me to cover up," she said, reaching for the one he offered. She let the champagne explain, "Don't pirates want their captives naked?"

"Pirates?" He chuckled.

"That's what you look like. All dark and intense. All that curly hair and those great teeth. I've even noticed an earring."

He reached for the bottle of champagne in her hand. She let him take it, but he didn't pour more for himself. Instead, he set the bottle behind his back where she couldn't reach it without climbing all over him.

And that idea was beginning to seem pretty damn good.

"You did this," she waved her hand to indicate the remains of their meal, "so I wouldn't have to stare at Philip's empty chair across from me. I read the brochure, you know. The first night's dinner is supposed to be formal, with expert service and five-star food."

He grinned and made her breath catch in her throat. The breath quickly turned into a tiny hiccup. "This was better," he said.

She smiled at him, watching his eyes. They were warm, caring and she liked his thick black lashes.

She sat with her back against the wall of the hot tub, her knees pulled up, her long skirt demurely over her knees to her feet. Now that she wore the pullover he'd given her she was covered but for her toes.

He kept staring at them as if he couldn't take his eyes away.

Experimentally, she dropped her knees to sit cross-legged, suddenly aware of the tight thong pressing against her clit.

She licked her lips.

His eyes flashed awareness and made her think of hot pools and rising steam. Her nipples tightened.

5

When Teri changed positions to sit cross-legged Jared nearly choked. What he wouldn't give to have Teri lift her skirt to her waist to show him that long, thin strip of thong. He could pull that strip out with his teeth and fill his mouth with her liquid heat. He could lap at her all he wanted, play all he wanted, kiss and lick and press against her all he wanted.

In his mind.

The last glass of champagne had obviously taken her past the point of clear decision and he had scruples. Scruples that wouldn't allow him to take advantage. Sparks or no sparks.

"This is his favorite," she said, indicating the plates that had just been cleared of duck and rice. She tilted her flute of champagne to her lips, but found it empty. She set the glass down slowly and deliberately with no comment.

"He told me we should be celibate before we married," she went on. "So I agreed. Always agreeable, that was Teri." She spoke with a wry bitterness and ended on a small chuckle at her own expense.

"Celibate? You?" There was no way a woman like Teri could

handle celibacy. Obviously, the fiancé was a wimp, not worth Teri's tears. In love with another woman and still going along with a wedding. Dickhead.

"He said he wanted to make these first few days of marriage special. It's known as revirginating . . ."—she picked up her flute again and peered into it as if expecting to see champagne where there was none a moment ago—"or revirginizing or something like that."

He snorted.

She laughed. "Exactly." She sighed long and hard. "I wanted this week to be perfect for him."

The imperiousness he'd heard had been stress and the desire to please this guy. The loser wouldn't have appreciated it. But that was something time and distance would teach her, so he kept his thoughts to himself.

For the first time, he saw her lip tremble. "*I* wanted to be perfect."

"You are," he said, surprised at the huskiness in his own voice.

She turned her face away, but kept her chin up as she stared off to the distance. Then her lip went from tremble to quiver in no time flat. He could see her blinking tears back and he had to admire her grit and honesty.

"June's twenty pounds overweight and blind as a bat and he chose *her*. So maybe I'm not perfect," she said, more to herself than to him, "not even close. But I'm honest, you know? And he should have been honest with me."

"Yes, he should have been." She was definitely past the point of clear thought. The best thing to do was let her blow off this steam.

She sniffed. "They've been boffing each other for the past six months and everyone knew it but me!" Her voice rose at the end and her pain spilled out.

There were no words to comfort her. He lifted his hands in

supplication but felt defeated by the glistening in her blue, blue eyes.

"What's wrong with me?" she asked in a little girl voice that tore at his gut.

"Nothing, there's nothing wrong with you. I think you're perfect." Jared grabbed a beach towel to wrap her in and opened his arms. With a little luck the towel would protect him from the charge he half-believed he imagined.

Teri crawled into his lap like a lost puppy needing warmth. Her tight little ass perched on his knee, her arms looped around his neck, her face tucked in under his chin. She smelled like sunblock lotion, woman and sunshine. Feminine and warm, she fit onto his lap as if she belonged there.

He slid his palm to one of his favorite places on a woman: the space below her waist that flared into lush rounded hips. One side of his hand held the bottom of her rib, the other, the top of her hip. The flare on Teri was perfectly proportioned, enticing and brought him to near pain, he wanted her so much. He tested her response with a slight squeeze. She snuggled closer, apparently content to let him explore.

The torture was exquisite. He was touching, but holding back, wanting but controlling it, smelling the scent of her skin and hair, but trying like hell not to.

He couldn't go any further than to offer a comforting lap and hug. Not when her breathing slowed, her head drooped and her arms felt like dead weight around his neck.

She'd fallen asleep.

Trusting, perfect Teri.

Shit.

A couple more minutes and he might have dismissed his thoughts of offering only comfort. Might have convinced himself that fucking a nearly unconscious woman who'd put on a fantastic display of sexual self-love deserved to be taken wherever and whenever he wanted.

Bullshit and he knew it.

He waited until her breathing eased and her head tried to slide out from under his chin. His buzzing chin. The towel had stopped the electric charge, but her head was in direct contact with his chin and throat. The whole area hummed.

Ignoring the sharp reminder, he decided she was asleep enough to be carried without waking. He took her down to the master cabin then stretched her out on top of the bed.

On contact she burrowed for the sheets. He pulled the coverlet over her from the other side of the bed and rubbed her covered shoulder to ease her fretful expression. Her left knee bent, her arms slid under the pillow and she released a soft champagne snore.

He sat at the side of the bed watching to be sure she didn't waken. So he could look his fill.

Look and think.

Damn.

This was it.

The men in his family were cursed. No matter how well they hid, no matter where they ran, their women found them.

With no more than a touch, the MacKay men were netted, gutted and filleted by these women. His brother had gone down without so much as a whimper in three days. His father had succumbed in under a week.

It had taken Jared less than an evening.

He might as well have taken his heart out and put it on her dinner plate with the duck and rice. Shit.

He was up against a monster problem, though. This fiancé could return, might come to his senses. Not to mention her feelings were still raw and open to persuasion. She must be confused, hurt, needy for reassurance.

Thank God there were no phones onboard. Unless Teri had

a cell, they would be out of contact with her world for the next seven days.

Was that enough time to convince her to stay and give up her Manhattan existence?

Her lips parted on a breath and he smiled. Heavy sleep turned her into a mouth breather. He smoothed his fingers through the ends of her hair to touch her, to feel her warmth and a little taste of the buzz.

The evening was still young, maybe she'd wake up again if the champagne wore off. He had work to do anyway and she may be creeped out if she knew he watched her sleep. He was still a virtual stranger.

He reluctantly left her side and headed above to clear away the dishes and leftover food before the seagulls swarmed the deck. The cries of the birds would disturb her sleep if not wake her completely.

Teri heard screeches. Philip's mother? About the place settings? Or was it the saleslady at the shoe store? "They fit! They fit! Buy! Buy! Bye-bye . . . Philip bye-bye . . ."

She swept her hair out of her face and sat up. She was still in her bathing suit, still on the *SandJack*, thank God, and still single, an even bigger thank God.

She'd been saved from making the biggest mistake of her life. She giggled, delighted with the cabin, delighted with her freedom, just delighted.

Jared. He must have carried her down here, tucked her in and left. She listened and heard nothing but the sea birds, the source of the screeches. Not Philip's mother, although she'd always seemed within a breath of screeching. Another wonderful thing. She wouldn't have that woman in her life.

Count your blessings, Teri.

She tugged off the pullover Jared had given her to wear and

undid her bathing suit top. Her breasts fell free. Relief. She rubbed the flesh under each one where the underwire had pressed against her all night. She usually slept nude and wasn't used to this kind of restriction.

Which may be the reason she'd woken so early. Dawn's light was pearly at the porthole, still pink-tinged. She slid out from under the coverlet and went to the bathroom to shower.

The rest of the *SandJack* was still, soundless. Jared must still be asleep.

She tiptoed into the bathroom, stepped out of her thong and into the shower. The water was hot, but there wouldn't be an endless supply onboard so she set it to warm and hurried through her routine.

The first morning of her time with the pirate. She pulled out a huge fluffy bath sheet and wrapped herself in it, controlling a small shiver of excitement. A narrow shelf over the toilet held bottles of body lotion, shampoo and conditioner. The scent Jared had chosen was exquisite. Sensual and spicy, the texture of the body lotion slick.

She filled her palm and massaged the cream into her breasts, bringing her nipples to peak. Jared's wicked smile filled her vision. She worked quickly on her arms and calves, but when it came to smoothing the cream into her upper thighs, she slowed, imagined Jared's hands there, at the crease between her mons and her leg.

She shook herself free of the sensuous fantasy and wrapped the towel around herself again.

There were still no sounds of life aboard. She'd make coffee. Surely the smell would wake him.

She crept out of the bathroom and turned into the kitchen. The coffee maker was timed to start in an hour, which gave her some idea of Jared's internal clock. But she needed caffeine now, especially after sleeping off all that champagne.

She canceled the timer and turned on the coffee. Just when she'd found the cupboard that held the mugs, Jared appeared in the doorway of his small cabin. He was sleep tousled, in a pair of swim trunks. His chest hair covered each nipple and thinned down to a point just above the waistband of his trunks.

She watched, fascinated by the hand he used to scrub across his belly. Fresh from sleep, he seemed unaware she was there. His sculpted chest called to her, his arms, both strong and smooth-looking, had held her last night when she needed holding more than anything.

He could have done so much more and she wouldn't have fought, wouldn't even have been capable of protesting. It warmed her that he'd realized she was beyond consent and that he'd been a gentleman about it. She had deliberately teased him, let him think she was ready, willing, and able. If he had taken what she'd so blatantly offered, she couldn't have blamed him.

But it pleased her no end that not only did her pirate have a heart, he had a good dose of gentlemanly scruples.

His hair, even blacker in the weak light, stuck up in adorable cowlicks around his forehead. He reached for the ceiling and stretched each sinuous muscle and his morning erection was obvious. And spectacular.

"Hello," she said.

He released the stretch. His gaze caught hers, then ran down her body to her bare legs and feet. "Hi. Sleep well?" He smiled, apparently delighted with what he'd seen.

"Like a drunken sailor."

He grinned. "You were that." He cocked an eyebrow at her and she realized she was still wrapped in the bath sheet.

She patted the knot sitting on her chest. "I thought I'd get the coffee on first, then get dressed."

"Don't have to dress on my account." His smile widened into pure come-get-me and she very nearly did.

The coffee burbled into the pot while she processed his comment. "No, I don't suppose I do. You could have undressed me last night, but you didn't."

He put up his hands in surrender. "And have you feel awkward this morning? No. You'd have had every right to demand to go back to Kingston and I want this time with you."

Her breath stalled. She couldn't speak.

Jared moved closer. "I want you to stay, Teri."

"I'd like that." She moved toward him, too.

"I want you." His voice curled around her, drew her near, pulled at her insides.

The sigh of the coffee maker punctuated the intensity of the moment. "I want you, too," she said, "for all the time I'm here."

He reached out and she closed her eyes, wanting to be swept into his embrace, wanting, needing the feel of his firm lips and hard arms.

But his touch didn't come. She opened her eyes to see him pluck a mug out of the cupboard behind her. He offered another to her. He brushed her fingers as she took it. The electric arc that had startled them so badly the first time passed between them again.

"Not so weird this time, eh?" he said as he traced her knuckle, wrapped around the mug handle.

"No, not scary, either."

He blinked and smiled in a mysterious way that set her heart to race. "I'm glad you're not frightened, Teri. I would never hurt you." He poured coffee into their mugs and took a drink.

She sipped her coffee too, and contemplated his words, his actions the evening before, his kind consideration for her raw feelings.

"I dreamed last night," she offered.

"No surprise there. About Philip?"

"I guess. I dreamed of freedom. I was flying at the bow of

the *SandJack*. When I woke up, I felt happier than I have in a long time. Philip betrayed me. June betrayed me. Being here and away from everyone asking questions is the best place for me." She touched his forearm, the black coarse hair springy under her fingertips, the flesh warm and alive. "This charge I feel when we touch is very odd."

"Yes." He grinned. "But it's growing on me."

"It makes me feel alive. But then, I dodged a bullet yesterday so it could just be relief."

"Could be, but that doesn't explain why I feel it, too." His grin widened. He brushed the back of his hand against her jaw, by her neck. "I'm glad you're relieved."

She tilted into the caress, closed her eyes and savored the tingle of understanding that danced between them. This time was apart, separate from her life at home. She'd take these days for what they were. Time to heal. Then she'd go home to begin again.

6

While Jared showered, Teri took the time to investigate the rest of the cupboards. She dug out some healthy looking grain bread and the toaster. Over the sink she found plates and cutlery, then she got butter out of the fridge under the counter.

The water stopped running so she pressed the lever on the toaster and poured him another mug of coffee. Handing it to him, she saw he'd done the same thing she had. He wore a bath towel tied at his waist. The intimacy of his choice struck her.

They were naked, but they weren't. They looked like people comfortable with a morning routine, but they weren't. They looked like people of long acquaintance, but they weren't.

What they were was attracted.

She decided to cut to the chase and undid the knot at her chest. Her bath sheet dropped, as did his jaw.

"You're exquisite." He moved his hand in a slow, palm up gesture that took her breath. She focused on his fingertips, stretching toward her, the supplication in the gesture making her belly quiver and her heart race. She saw the calluses, the evidence of his labor-intensive day, but she already knew the gentleness in them. In him.

Without speaking Jared was asking permission to touch, to feel her skin, to caress, to take her places she'd never been. He let his hand hover near her neck, as if she might break if he allowed the full force of his desire to flow. His fingers actually trembled in her peripheral vision. She knew why.

He knew the arc would come again. They drew sparks of energy from each other, but she was too far gone to care. Whatever it was made her hot and yearn for him. Only him.

"There's no stopping if I touch you, Teri."

"I know." She closed her eyes, tilted her head back to let him see her neck, the way the blood pulsed in a mad rush to her head. "This is exactly what I need." *And what I need to hear.*

When his touch came, her flesh burned.

His fingers seared and scorched and sent an inferno down her spine. He cupped the back of her head to hold her when she couldn't have moved if she'd tried.

His kiss was slow, easy, undemanding for a long time. He explored her lips, her soft inner skin, the ridge of her front teeth. She shuddered against his chest, raised her palms to cup his pecs, molded his shoulder muscles.

She squared her hips to his, felt the bulk of his bath sheet between them. But a languid sense of time slowing took her to a peaceful easing. There was lots of time to undo that knot, lots of time to explore and play and be together. To come together in every sense of the phrase.

The electric charge they felt eased back to a hum, a steady throbbing hum that grew and pulsed with life. Their life forces joined, melded and captured them.

His skin smelled of the men's body wash she'd seen in the shower. Spicy, heated by his body. Blood whooshed to her loins, every nerve tingled, every pulse pounded between her

legs. That whole secret place filled with moist heat and yearning. She felt herself soften in readiness, ripen for him. Drip for
him.

As he also prepared for her. To enter, to plunder, to take her.
His cock rose against her belly, pressing the roughness of the
terry cloth into her flesh.

And still, this was just a kiss. A first kiss, a tentative kiss, an
exploration of the attraction between them. A test.

His hands burrowed into her hair, cupped her head, massaged her scalp as he took and took and took from her lips. She
gave, and took back, swept up in the moment, in the exciting
electricity that was Jared.

His lips eased from hers, traced her jaw, trailed down her
neck, back up to her ear. His breath there sent powerful surges
down her spine that bloomed deep inside her most private
places.

"This is . . . so . . ." she trailed off, not sure she could believe
what it was she'd been about to say.

"Right?" He suggested. He pulled back, searched her eyes,
held her loosely, ready even now to step back if she needed him
to.

"Yes." Unbelievably, it was. So right.

He opened his towel, let it fall. His erection, heavy and jut-
ting, made her mouth go dry and her clit, plump and rosy, pulse
with need.

She pulled herself up to sit on the counter. Arching back-
ward, Teri offered herself. She expected him to prod at her entrance, to rush to her core, to plunder where he could, like the
pirate he was.

She propped herself on stiff arms, tilted her head back so her
hair hung like a fall behind her, the tips grazing the countertop.
She couldn't make more of an offering than this. Vulnerable,
open, her arms behind her, her legs spread to receive, her head

thrown back. She could hear his labored breath, feel the arc of pulsing need, smell the arousal of her own flesh, sense the import of the act of possession.

"Do it." She was braced and ready.

"Teri," his voice held wonder, excitement, intimacy. "Look at me."

She raised her head, opened one eye. He stood transfixed.

"I've never seen a more beautiful woman, a more beautiful offering than this. But I need you to look at *me.* I need you to know who's inside you."

She nodded, befuddled. "Okay."

"What's my name?"

"Jared."

"Who am I?" The demand in his voice was raw-edged, the words bitten off and harsh.

"Jared MacKay, captain of the *SandJack*."

"What am I?"

"My pirate."

He blinked when he heard the words. His face softened. When he looked at her again, she thrilled at what she saw in his gaze. She'd offered whatever he wanted sexually, made it plain he could do anything he liked.

He dropped to his knees. Oh, he liked *that*. . . . Thank you, thank you, she said in a silent plea. A flash of the actors crossed her mind's screen and she shivered in anticipation of the touch of his tongue on her moist slit. Would it be powerful like a ravishing pirate or gentle and coaxing like a tentative lover?

His long, callused fingers gripped her ankle, held her foot still.

She felt his mouth on her big toe and jerked, startled. But he held her foot still and moved on to the next toe. Fire raced up her leg from each touch of his tongue and set a throb to start inside. Pulsing and needy she bloomed for him as he set sparklers on each toe, giving each equal attention.

"Oh, Jared, that's exquisite."

"I've wanted to kiss these tiny perfect toes since you took your shoes off at the pier."

"Just keep moving up my leg and I'll be happy."

His fingers slid to her knee. "You mean up to here?" He swirled her pinky toe into his mouth and tugged on it.

Her knee turned into a fireworks display at the same time her toe melted in his mouth. "Unnnnhh, higher." She'd implode if he kept up this slow pace.

His fingers swirled behind her knee and probed delicately there, making her croon in desperation for him to move higher, but she knew asking him would only prolong the agony. He wanted to torture her.

"I didn't know you were a tease," she murmured.

"Unlike yourself?" The husky tone held humor, but she was too far gone to get the joke.

She counted the inches he crept. Two, then three, four . . .

This was not what she expected. He ran a finger along her sole, sending shudders up her leg to her heart.

And then it came to her. "Is this payback for my game on deck with the lotion?"

He raised himself to lean over her, desire and deep humor blazing from his eyes. "Did you think I didn't want my tongue on you? Your finger was less than an inch from your clit. You threw your head back and the sun played across your skin in pink and red and I couldn't tell if it was my eyes playing tricks or if you really were on fire."

"I'm on fire now," she said hoping beyond reason that he'd quench her and do it fast.

But his mouth quirked up into an evil, teasing grin and she knew down to her well-sucked toes, she was at his mercy.

The pirate took complete control.

7

Teri considered being at Jared's mercy and wasn't sure she liked the idea. He was so damn *slow*, when all she wanted was to get to it. Besides, she'd decided at first sight the man needed to learn some manners.

She grabbed his head, pulled him down fast and kissed his smile hard. She plunged her tongue into his mouth, sucked his bottom lip, licked the tip of his tongue until she couldn't take any more. She moaned. It had been so long, and she'd been so lonely. Lonely in her bed, lonelier in her heart.

She fell back to the countertop, startled by the surge of desire that had her demand more than he wanted to give. Six months. Six long months since she had felt . . .

Her hands on Jared's chest, tempted beyond reason, she squeezed his pecs, wanting him to understand. *To get it.* "I haven't had sex in six months. Hurry!"

He stopped kissing her neck immediately, loosened his grip. "Excuse me?"

"I was hoping for faster."

He quirked an eyebrow. "No can do. I think the wattage on the buzz drops when we go slow."

She shuddered at the throaty sound of his voice. "I'm so horny I'm squirming."

He closed his eyes, set his jaw so hard she saw a muscle jump. "If I move faster it'll be over before you're ready. Believe me, slow will work."

Suddenly she realized he wanted fast, too, but he was more concerned with giving her a sure thing. She melted. "You're in charge, Jared. We'll go slow this time."

Her statement took the edge off, assuring her that now that they were here together, their bodies ready, their minds set, the end would be spectacular. And spectacular beat fast every time.

She smiled to ease him and pecked Jared on the lips. "You should know Philip's completely gone," she patted her chest over her heart.

"Glad to hear it." His eyes glowed relief and happiness. "Now that there are only two of us here, let's move to the bed." He slid his hands down her arms to her hands and tugged.

She moved off the counter and felt the dip as he swung her up into his arms. She'd never been carried before. "I like this," she said. "My pirate's carrying me off to a ravishment."

"Prepare yourself, then. I'm definitely not stopping now."

She laughed and set her lips to his earlobe as he walked.

"Yes, yes, yes," she breathed into his ear. "Ravish me, take me, all of me, all over."

He followed her down onto the bed and she fell into a warm cocoon of heat and desire and longing where for the first time in too long, she wasn't alone.

"Before things get any more interesting, I'm going to have to leave you here," he said. "I put the condoms away in the bathroom cabinet."

Jared had another reason for going slow. She was tiny in

spite of her taut athletic build. He was far too aroused for her comfort.

Seeing her timid expression when he returned, he knew he would have to ease into her. But, he would get into her, of that he was sure, because under the timidity he read hunger that matched his own.

She rolled to her side, propped her head on her elbow and patted the bed in invitation. He settled next to her. He slid his arm under her head so she could snuggle into him then slowly petted her smooth warm thigh. He traced her flushed skin from knee to crotch, where he found her dewy curls. His fingers combed through them.

She bit her lip. "That's nice. The buzz goes straight inside."

Smiling, he kissed the top of her head.

She ran a palm from his waist to his shoulder. "Take me somewhere hot, Jared, somewhere steamy," she said. "But take me slow."

He shuddered at the thought of having her for a week. Of all the things he'd do to make her want to stay. Stretching her arms over her head, he held her wrists by one hand. He coaxed her to lie flat, set out for him like a feast.

He fed.

He fed on her neck, her ears, licked her collarbones, making sure to dip into the hollow at the base of her throat. Her neck was warm and smelled of heaven and promise. Her breasts were full, lush, tipped with nipples that tasted of candy and sugar. He sucked on her deeply, coaxing her to stay still by weighing her down with a leg thrown over hers. When she moaned low in her throat, he stopped.

"No, no sounds, no movement, Teri. If you want slow you have to help me. If I feel you respond, if I feel you want me, I'll go too fast, too hard, too soon. I'll take, Teri, I'll take and take and take. And you've given enough."

She nodded, but didn't speak, although her eyes spoke volumes. She wanted him, but he put the thought out of his head. This had to be about Teri receiving. As much as she said her heart was free, she'd been through a shock and she needed time.

When she'd been filled up again, when she felt whole again, he could take. She would be strong enough then.

He slid down her body and kissed her thigh. Working his way down past her knee, skimming along her calf he spent considerable time licking her fine-boned ankle. Then he moved on to the arch of her instep. It was when he licked her big toe and took it into his mouth that she squealed.

She thrashed on the bed until he quieted her by placing his palm over her vulva. She was wet, nearly dripping. When he pressed lightly, she moaned.

"Let it go, Teri. You need to come, deep and hard, and I'll take you there now."

"Yes, please." She opened her legs wider to accommodate the full width of his hand.

He pressed against her clitoris and rubbed gently but steadily. A sigh of satisfaction signaled her acceptance of the attention. Her thighs tightened and her knees bent as she began to press up into his hand.

Gauging her ready for more, he slid his thumb into her cleft and felt her inner walls clasp him tight. If she was this snug on his thumb she'd be heaven on his shaft. He eased his thumb halfway out and her hips responded by following, reaching for him. He obliged and slid back in with a circling motion that made her croon encouragement.

His erection burned like fire so he pressed himself between the bed and her plump, soft ass. He wanted to push to ease himself a little, but her skin felt so good on his he was afraid he'd shoot if he moved.

Teri began to pump in response to his thumb movement, the

scent of her nearly making him crazy. He heard the slick sounds from her cleft, felt her sticky juices sliding across her turgid clit and knew he had to taste.

"You'll come now. In my mouth."

She moaned and nodded. "Yes, yes . . ."

He slid to his knees in front of her, lifted her ass and buried his face in her incredible pussy. Wet, open, ready, Teri tasted like pearls of delicious ambrosia. Her delicate inner lips quivered on his tongue while her clit plumped and protruded from her hood. He sucked on her heavy clit and swirled his tongue around it while she squirmed and bucked and with a sudden cry, came.

Her thighs trembled, her juices flowed and her back arched, pressing her up to his face for more and more and more. . . .

He held her there until the quivers subsided, then lapped at her gently to bring her back down to earth.

When he looked at her face, he saw tears tracking down her cheeks. She swiped at them, not wanting him to see, then she reached for his face to bring him to her for a kiss. He didn't mention the tears, they were hers and hers alone.

"Thank you," she said after a long exploration of his mouth. "You have no idea how much I needed that."

She ran her hand down his chest and finally set her fine delicate fingers to his cock. She circled him and slid from the base to his tip and he felt the squeeze as she sought to measure him. Her eyes went wide at the fullness of him.

"I'll ease in slowly. I'll be careful."

"Like hell you will," she said and playfully pushed him to his back on the bed.

She moved smooth as a mermaid in water as she rose over him, hand still grasping him, sliding and building tension that threatened to spill all over her hand.

She wet her lips and gave him a glance that burned through

to his heart. She dipped her head and all he could see was the top of her blond head, all he could feel was the silk of her hair spreading across his thighs and low belly.

Teri moved her hand lower to cup his sac and he nearly shouted with the exquisite heat of her weighing him. He knew his cock was near her mouth, but he couldn't see anything. He lifted her hair away, twined it in his fingers until he got a great view of her perfect, wet lips as they descended on his straining head.

Just before contact she squeezed more pre-come from him and he watched her tongue as it reached out to taste his slickness.

"Mm, that's delicious," she said when she drew her tongue back into her mouth to swirl his flavor across her taste buds. "Oh, yeah . . ."

She tilted back down to him and he had to slam his head back and arch off the bed with the intense, gradual taking of his cock into her mouth. She paused and he felt her open more as she slid down his length.

After that, he lost track of how far into her throat he went, amazed at her talent for head. Such a little woman, such a deep throat . . .

She sucked and nibbled his length before going back to his sac, but eventually he had to tug her away. "I don't want to come this way. I need to be inside you this time." The first time.

Teri smiled and surprised him again by straddling him. Then she raised herself and squatted over him. From this position he could see her pussy, open and streaming moisture. He looked so big in comparison to her tidy, tight opening. Too big to fit. *Damn.*

She reached for a condom packet and tore it open, taking the decision out of his hands. He wanted to go slow, he wanted more than anything not to hurt her, but she made him crazy with need.

He loved that the tip of her tongue came out in a delicious

little point as she focused on rolling the condom on. "There," she said, "safe now."

"I don't want to hurt you. Are you sure you can manage this?"

She circled him and squeezed, measuring his girth. "I've never been so ready in my life."

The exquisite sensations Teri felt as she pressed herself onto his immense erection made her inner muscles quake. She leaned forward over him so he could suckle her breasts as she slid down the length of him, slowly opening and accepting him. As Jared laved each of her breasts and sucked them into his mouth she began to rock against him. Her clit finally made contact with his pubis and she could go no farther. She settled for a moment, allowing her channel to accept the fullness of him before she moved on him again. Rockets of desire rolled through her, right out her legs and arms, down to her fingertips and toenails.

She shuddered and closed her eyes to better appreciate and thrill to the sensuality of his cock. Jared had no idea how far the magnificence of that first filling could take a woman.

Exquisite tension built as she slowly accepted the length and width of him.

She gave an experimental roll and buck and shook with the erotic pleasure that volcanoed up from her low belly. Another roll, another shot of pleasure. She planted her hands on his shoulders and moved faster. "Oh, yes!"

Jared's neck arched as he tried to slow her quickening pace, but she didn't want control. She wanted wild abandon so she let loose with a cry of ecstasy.

"Fast!" She pleaded.

Suddenly she was riding a rocket as Jared responded with a loss of control that thrilled her. He pushed and strained up into her. Then he grabbed her ass and lifted her to slide up and down his cock, setting an even faster pace. She squealed with the joy of finally getting what she wanted, needed, craved.

His wild bucking took her over the edge. With another keening cry, Teri came again, arching and rocking over him.

Just as the stars receded from her eyes, she felt Jared pump and flex against her inner walls as he spurted into her, hot and streaming.

She milked him by squeezing and releasing her thighs to ride him out. His orgasm brought on another for her so she pressed against his pubis and held on, straining.

Jared pressed slowly, oh so gently against her vulva with his thumb and helped carry her along. This orgasm built into an exquisite peak in such a measured way that when she came, gushing against his hand, she was nearly taken by surprise.

The sensation wracked her body and she knew no one but Jared would ever make her feel this way.

Teri lifted her arms in a victory stretch. "Yes! Yes! Yes! I knew it could be great. I knew it!"

Jared laughed with her, rolled her beneath him. The deep affection she read in his gaze before he kissed her gently, completely, left her breathless and wondering.

A goner, that's what he was. His life as he knew it was over. Having Teri had been awesome and he wanted more. He wanted all of her. The charge from touching her had settled permanently around his heart.

He mentally tallied the days he had left. Down to five. But it was still too soon to talk about longer. He had to give her the honeymoon she craved, the time she needed and most of all he needed to help her see that her life had changed as well.

As strongly as he felt the buzz, she did, too. She just didn't know what it meant yet.

He could tell her about the MacKay family curse and how his brother and father had succumbed, but she'd think he was crazy. Or worse. She might accuse him of having some kind of obsessive stalker mentality. If Teri settled on that explanation he wouldn't have a chance of getting through to her.

He knew a quiet cove that was hidden from most casual observers and headed for it. The *SandJack* responded the way she always did, smoothly and instantly. They'd be anchored before dusk.

Once anchored in the cove, Jared would have Teri to himself and they'd learn so much about each other that she'd never want to leave.

That was as far ahead as he could look. Because if this didn't work, if Teri kept to her plan to return to her life, he knew he had a long, lonely future ahead of him. There'd never be another Teri. Not for him.

He'd settled once for a woman he thought suited him well. Had waited for the love between them to grow, but instead of growing, the mild affection they'd had slipped away, ground down by the rat race of corporate life.

His decision to pursue a life on the *SandJack* had killed the last of the marriage.

If this charge he felt with Teri was the real thing, she'd be more than happy to join him aboard the *SandJack* and would see the value in living free.

All he had to do was convince his tightly wound, tightly focused, tightly built piece of woman that life could be lived loose.

Jared MacKay was more than up for the challenge.

8

Teri slid the hot baking pan onto the counter, pleased with how the brownies looked. She'd baked the recipe from memory and had had her doubts about how they would turn out.

"What's that incredible smell?" Jared's head appeared in the rectangle of sky in the hatch.

"Fudge brownies. Would you like one?" She laughed at the speed of his descent into the galley. She'd learned some proper nautical terms in the two days she'd been onboard.

He grabbed a knife and let it hover over the cooling pan. "How soon can we cut them?"

"Do you want frosting or not?"

"Depends. If I say yes will that take longer?"

"They'll have to cool completely before I frost them."

"Then no. I have appetites that must be seen to." He waggled an eyebrow and waved the knife with a pendulum's accuracy.

She patted his behind then gave it a squeeze. "I thought we'd been doing a fine job of handling your appetites." And hers.

They'd only taken a break from exploring their incredible sexual connection because she was sore.

Besides, she'd become increasingly interested and curious about her pirate and he seemed quite happy to share everything about himself and his life. They'd agreed it was time to find out more about each other as people.

Her nerves had jumped at the idea of sharing some of her innermost thoughts and dreams, so she'd taken refuge in baking. It was an old remedy, comforting and relaxing and one she hadn't indulged in for far too long.

Watching Jared's impatience for the brownies to cool brought a secret joy back to life in her chest. His eagerness to sample the brownies delighted her and silly as it was, it warmed her to see his enthusiasm for something so simple.

She waved her hand over the pan to see how much heat remained. "They're still too warm, but we could take them upstairs."

"On deck."

"On deck. We could take them on deck to cool faster. Hey, at least I know it's a head and not a bathroom now. And this is the galley." She waved her arms to encompass the compact cooking area.

He tested the side of the pan gingerly. She passed him two potholders, picked up the knife and followed him and her pan of brownies to the deck.

He held the pan out to the breeze and sniffed appreciatively. "How long?"

"Remind me to hide the next thing I bake until it's ready."

"No." He tested the side of the pan again and dropped the potholders to the deck. "It's cooler already."

"You, Jared MacKay, are a baby." But she'd found another reason to like him. "I haven't baked for someone as greedy as you in a long time."

"I can't believe it. Every man in my family has a soft spot for women who bake. I thought all men did. You know, all that stuff about a way to a man's heart."

"Let's just say I haven't had reason to bake for a long time."

"Fair enough."

"This little cove is beautiful," she said, shading her eyes to take her first look around their private destination. A short stretch of beach beckoned but she could see even from here that the drop-off immediately off shore was deep. "But the swimming looks treacherous."

"Better to swim off the swim grid in the stern."

She turned and looked to where she expected open sea. But there was none. Just more land and beach.

"Where are we?"

"Seclusion Cove. Not very original, I know, but the name says it all. You can't see the entrance to the cove until you're on top of it and most larger boats pass by. As do the charters."

"Would you have brought us here if things were different?"

"No. I want this to be a place you remember as ours. Just ours." He stood behind her and looped his arms across her chest in a light hug. His broad back protected hers from the sun while he pointed out some of the flowers and plants.

"There's sea grape," he said, pointing out a tall, dense tree with broad leaves. "I've got some jam made from the grapes."

"Can we pick some?" They didn't look much like the grape vines she'd seen in vineyards.

"They're too tart to eat fresh. They grow high here because the cove's sheltered from the wind."

The flora and fauna were interesting, but the large, rather insistent erection she felt pressing into her back was by far more enthralling. She reached behind her and cupped him, giving him a light, firm squeeze from root to tip. He bit her earlobe in response.

Shivers of anticipation ran from her ear to her loins where they settled into a burn. Jared continually surprised her with his appetite for sex. She matched him in every way, and that shocked her even more.

"I want to eat you," he murmured against her ear.

"Me? Or my brownies?" she murmured back, feeling his hot finger explore her curls. She leaned forward and stepped wide for him, unable to quench her rising fire without his deep touch.

"Can't I have both?"

She laughed. "The brownies should be cool enough now, but I'm getting hotter," she said.

"You're confusing me." His hands went palm up as if weighing his decision. "Brownies." His left hand moved. "Or Teri." His right hand moved.

She laughed. "Once the brownies are gone, they're gone. But I'll be here for a while longer."

He growled into her ear. "Brownies it is."

He pulled away and she felt bereft at the change in temperature. But when she turned she had to laugh again at his silent demand for the knife she'd laid on top of the pan of brownies.

She presented the knife to him like an operating room nurse. A quick slap into his hand and a precision slice later and he had a quarter of the brownies in his hand.

"I offered you one brownie as I recall."

"This is one."

She rolled her eyes.

"Would you like me to cut you a piece, too?" he asked.

"A small one. By your standards, minuscule."

"I remember how brownies are supposed to look," he said, cutting a much smaller square for her. "It's just been years since I've had a homemade one, so I'm not going to apologize for being greedy. You make me that way."

She thought of the great sexual appetite he'd aroused in her and she understood. "Deprivation can release the inner glutton for many things. Sex included."

She accepted the brownie he offered and tasted it. "Oh, this is good, I thought I'd forgotten the recipe, but I guess it's like riding a bike."

He gathered her into his arms again and resumed the position they'd taken at the deck railing. Quiet and secluded, the cove was a paradise where there was no evidence that man existed.

The heat of Jared at her back comforted her more than it should. The man himself comforted her more than she should allow but she couldn't see any harm in pretending they were a couple for the time she was aboard.

"So, you were serious. You don't bake in New York?" His voice at her ear startled her.

"No time. And my kitchen's so tiny, it's a hassle."

"But the galley has to be smaller and you managed just fine."

"It's different here. More relaxed. Vacations are for doing all the things you enjoy but don't have time for, right?"

"Right."

"Besides, Philip didn't like me to bake. Said I'd eat it all and gain weight. Being short means even a small weight gain's a problem."

Jared snorted. "Not for me. I like a woman who enjoys life enough to live it without guilt."

She wondered if she'd ever be able to get completely clear of the doubts Philip had raised in her. She wasn't sure, but Jared was certainly helping.

She felt him press against her lower back and smiled at the rising erection that prodded her. No matter that they'd agreed, reluctantly, to give themselves a few hours to recuperate from the sex marathon they'd indulged in, he was obviously ready for more.

"You looked happy when you tossed your shoes overboard at the dock. What was that about?" he asked.

"Oh, that." She didn't want to talk about Philip, but too much of her life had revolved around him and his demands. Maybe talking it out would exorcize the last remaining irritants he'd foisted onto her psyche.

"Yeah, that. I thought women were psychologically unable to throw away shoes. Any shoes."

She laughed. "It was a small rebellion. Philip thought I looked too short next to him. He likes women with long legs so I tried to, you know, emphasize them."

"Asshole."

"To be fair, that wasn't the only reason I use stilettos. I'm in a very competitive position and I want to get ahead. Women my height can sometimes have difficulty being seen as authoritative. When you're under five-foot-four you're not an automatic 'go-to,' more of a 'go-fer.' And I hate that! I hate that I have to be smarter, tougher, faster than everyone around me just to be noticed."

"Sounds hard on the ego."

"The talent gets to have ego. Production assistants get coffee and muffins."

He made a dismissive noise in his throat she read as impatience. "Enough about my career. Let's get back to our vacation."

"Let's get back to your legs. Your perfect legs. They're exactly long enough to wrap around my waist, which is all you really need. And I love your toes."

She stretched out her right leg, flexed her foot to show him her bare toes. "Really?"

"I thought I'd already shown you." He nuzzled her neck where it met her shoulder. She giggled. He knew she was ticklish there.

His erection was huge by now, so again, she slid her hand up behind her and clasped him. His sharp intake of breath pleased her. He was always so ready, so fun to play with and tantalize.

He turned her and they shared a kiss that tasted of fudge brownie and each other. Oh, so decadent.

When he released her she sank to her knees, wanting to put the chocolate flavor that still lingered all over his glorious cock.

When she moved in to take him into her mouth, he stepped back.

"Not yet, let's go for a swim." He untied her bikini bottom. It fell and she stepped out of it, lifting her hair so he could undo her bra top. The breeze raised her nipples to buds. He lingered for a moment while he rubbed his thumb across them, bringing an exquisite thrumming to life.

Moisture pooled inside her. "I can't believe how wet you make me with just a touch."

"I can't get enough of you. One week won't be enough."

"It will have to be." But in her heart, she agreed.

9

Teri saw a mischievous grin on Jared's face just before he lifted her into his arms. She squeaked in mock fear. This was another new thing for her to discover: play, sexual and otherwise.

He carried her to the swim grid off the stern and chucked her, laughing and naked, into the water. He stripped off his swim trunks and dived in.

Skinny-dipping in the Caribbean was something she would never have done before. They played together like dolphins and she made sure to keep just out of his reach. In a mood like this, she couldn't tell what her pirate might do.

After a few minutes of splashing and water tag, she surfaced to find herself alone. Somewhere in the back of her mind she heard the heavy, thrumming tune to *Jaws* and knew Jared was probably under her right now watching her kick lazily to stay afloat.

She looked down just as Jared swam up the length of her in a rush of bubbles. He grabbed her as she screamed in delight.

The warm water made their skin slick and slippery as he held her close. His chest hair teased at her nipples. He raised her a little so her breasts bobbed on the surface between them. He reached for one with his mouth and she moved closer, letting the thrill of his mouth arrow to her sex.

His cock stirred against her thigh and she warmed immediately. She slid her legs around his hips, hoping to entice him inside.

Rivulets of water cascaded from his face to his chest where the droplets caught in the hair, like diamonds. He lifted her, pressed his face between her breasts and blew a raspberry against her chest, making her laugh.

Before she knew what he was doing, he raised her to float on the surface and began suckling her breasts again.

"Mm, salty," he said, while rolling a nipple with his tongue. "Do you taste like this all over?"

"I have no idea—you'll have to find that out for yourself," she teased, feeling her moisture gather for him.

He continued his ministrations on her breasts, all the while breaking into murmurs of what he was planning for later. "Long, slow kisses," he said, making her moan. "A little exploring with my fingers," he added, "to see how deep you are, how wet you become."

She sighed, trying to think of something she could add to the conversation, but he wouldn't give her time to think. She floated under the sun of the warm Caribbean Sea listening to his deeply erotic voice, with the lap of the water at her center. She drifted, aware only of the sensation of freedom and arousal.

Fingers brushing her curls, small wavelets dancing against her, his heated voice against her ear, caused tremors of desire to run through her.

She glanced down, saw his hand between her thighs, creating the little waves that crashed against her shore. "Oh, Jared, touch me," she pleaded. "This isn't enough."

He brought her down to line up against him in the water and she felt his rigid erection against her belly.

"Here?" she asked, preparing to lift her legs around his waist.

"No, here," he said and hoisted her onto the swim grid. Lifting her legs over his shoulders, he buried his head between her thighs and set to work opening her with his lips and tongue. "Mm, you're delicious this way," he said.

She braced her hands behind her and spread her thighs, giving him everything he sought. He sucked her clit into his mouth and she thought she would die with the ecstasy, tumble into the water and give in to the wild feel of him. But she held on, not wanting to miss one iota of what he was doing. His tongue entered her over and over again while his fingers, oh, his fingers did marvelous things.

She shuddered again and again until she cried out, "Enough! I can't take anymore."

She managed to peek at him and was stunned by the beauty of his expression. He was enjoying himself as much as she was and she realized that for him, sex was a give-give thing.

And that was unfair.

"Please, you've got to let me taste you now. Right now," she said firmly, scrambling to the side so he could climb aboard.

"I like it when you're bossy," he said with a wicked grin. He hoisted himself onto the swim grid and settled himself on the open hatchway, displaying his cock like a flag. It was long and think and darkly veined. But the head was magnificently thick and powerful-looking. It looked exactly the way it felt inside her.

Swiping her tongue across his tip, she found him briny and hotter than the warm Caribbean seawater. His cock rose even farther when she wrapped her fingers around it. Taking the fully engorged tip into her mouth, she laved at him.

She played and teased and explored him. His reactions as she lapped and nipped and sucked made her feel powerful. She felt free, unrestricted.

She'd never had so much fun giving head. Jared was a relaxed, playful lover who let her indulge her every whim. She could do whatever she wanted, play in whatever way she pleased.

She traced the veins to their base and sucked each of his balls into her mouth until he groaned. She could tell he was trying to hold back and it was fun to drive him to the brink over and over again.

She felt more in control than she ever had and it was a heady experience to know she could bring a powerful man to his knees just with her mouth. She loved the experience, wanted it again and again. Wanted Jared again and again.

Finally giving him one more surging suck, she turned around and straddled his thighs, placing him at her entrance.

"Watch," she said. She opened herself and took the tip of him inside. Raising herself again, she released him. Again, she took him, a little farther in this time and spread her cheeks so he could see the penetration. He bucked against her.

"No. You can't move. Not until I say so." Again, she rose, denying him the soft wetness he so obviously craved.

He grabbed her cheeks and spread them himself this time. "More," he said hoarsely. "I want to see you take all of me."

First, she slid along the length of him, then pressed his tip against her, nearly coming right then. But she had to hang on, had to do for him what he'd done for her. Shaking with need she finally, slowly reached down and guided him into her, spreading herself as wide as she could to take him completely inside. Oh so slowly she slid down to his root and sat for a quiet moment so they could both catch their breath.

Squeezing her inner muscles, she began to milk him, her own slickness easing the way. She glanced over her shoulder at him. His eyes were closed, his teeth gritted and his jaw locked in his fight to control his flexing.

Taking pity on him, Teri began to move up and down his shaft, moistening herself and him until the slide became slick and hot and easy. Deeper and deeper he thrust as he could control himself no more. He drove into her with a power that took her breath away. Pumping like a piston, Teri cried out her own release as he plunged ever higher into her and exploded inside her.

Exhausted and drained, they stumbled into the cabin together and collapsed on the bed, entwined like longtime lovers.

A great sense of peace flowed through Teri every time they made love. She was happier right now, in the arms of this virtual stranger, than she had ever been before in her life. It was scary to have come so close to hooking up with a man who never made her feel this way. She'd had a frighteningly close call, and it had taken Jared almost no time to help her see it.

For that, she would be forever grateful. She slid her leg up and over his, luxuriating in the feel of his crisp leg hair and the hard feel of his shin bones under his flesh. His knees were knobby and masculine, his thighs long and ropy with strength.

Content to twirl a curl of his chest hair with a fingertip, she snuggled, secure in her place with him.

This was what sex was supposed to be, she realized. Loving should be relaxed, joyful, not a series of instructions or comments about everything she was doing wrong. It should not be squeezed in between meetings and late night phone calls to stressed-out, demanding Hollywood PR people.

Jared tucked Teri's head under his chin. She nestled there, content as they watched the sun dip below the treetops of their private cove.

Jared pleased himself by running his fingers through her drying hair. Teri was everything he wanted. She was funny, playful and loved to experiment. And she was brave.

He chuckled.

She lifted her face to look at him. "What?"

"You should have seen the wild look on your face when you

threw your shoes overboard. What a rebel." He'd bet a month's worth of charters that she'd never done anything so rebellious before in her life.

"I've never thought of myself as a rebel. But it felt good. Those shoes cost a small fortune, and I ran all over Manhattan before I found them."

He chuckled and tucked her head under his chin. He cuddled her close.

"Do you feel the hum? It's still here, but softer." She ran her hand down his chest, trailing sparks under his skin.

"Yes, softer, like a gentle current through my veins. Strangest damn thing."

"But I like it. It's warm and comfortable."

"Now it is because we just came. But after awhile it seems to build up to a higher charge." He wasn't sure if this thing ever fully went away. He made a mental note to check with his brother. Maybe after a decade or so things would calm down.

She nodded. "You make me feel alive in a way I've never experienced."

The MacKay curse affected the women in the same way, then. He ran his thumb from her wrist to her elbow. "Feel the trail?"

"Yes." She sighed and flung a leg over his. He felt the curls at the apex of her thighs against his hip. She was snugged in tight.

"I'm trying to process this whole thing," she said softly. "I've never even had a one-night stand and here I am, fucking my brains out with a man I'll never see again."

"Feeling guilty?" He tilted her head with a fingertip so he could see her eyes.

"That's why I'm processing. I don't feel guilty and that surprises me." She looked away again but he'd already seen what he wanted to see. She was being more open and more giving of herself all the time.

"I'm a small-town girl," she said. "Solid, Midwest roots. So it's weird that instead of feeling guilt, I feel as if this is exactly right."

"So if you're not originally from New York, where did you grow up?"

"Kansas, definitely small-town. I went to New York after college and fell into a great job, but it's really high pressure. I work for a morning show as a production assistant. There's a promotion looming and I've been working my butt off to get it. I think I'm in the lead. That's why I only booked a week off work for the wedding."

"And if you get the promotion, will you have more time to bake?"

"No." She frowned. "And now that I'm single again, I won't be able to move into a bigger place, either. My life's going to be even more frantic than before. Frantic but better."

"Better how?"

She tilted her head, gave him an odd expression and said, "Obviously you haven't spent a lot of time with someone who makes you feel inadequate."

"Why choose him?"

She shrugged. "He had all the qualifications. My family approved the marriage, almost making up for my decision to desert them. He's a lawyer, automatically putting him in the 'good catch' category."

Jared wondered what category a Caribbean gypsy would fall into and decided it would be "worst catch."

"So throwing your shoes into the drink wasn't your first rebellion."

She went still. "For the most part, I've lived quietly. Never wanted to make waves or worry people. Except for the move to New York, I've pretty much gone along with what everyone thinks is best for me."

"So when this lawyer showed up, the family felt you'd been saved from your own foolishness?"

"Ah! You know my parents."

"Most folks want their daughters secure rather than free. A big-time New York lawyer could provide a measure of security."

"I have four locks on my apartment door and they were my choice, not his. From now on I plan to be free rather than safe. This time with you has changed the way I see things. When I get home, my life will be different. *I* will be different."

"But you'll keep the locks?"

"Of course." She smiled. "Don't look so worried. I'm always careful." She seemed excited about returning to her hectic life, so he bided his time about asking her to stay. She wasn't ready to think about sharing her life with anyone yet.

"I appreciate your kindness in allowing me free use of the galley and . . . ah, how do I put this so it'll sound right?" Her hesitation said a lot about the direction of her thoughts.

He sat up and tugged her to sit in his lap. "You're not going to thank me for the sex, are you?" Her weak smile made him shake his head. "I'm not offering pity sex. I wanted you even before I knew you'd be here alone."

"Really?"

"Don't know how I would have handled things if you were married. I don't hustle married women but I'd have been tempted."

She laughed. "Do tell." She looped her arms around his neck, her weight on his lap feather-light.

"You had me at first sight, marching down the dock in those ridiculous shoes, with your fine tight ass and the fire blazing in your eyes."

She made a face of total disbelief. "You were napping."

"Like hell I was. My dick jumped to life and my mouth went dry when you turned around to get your luggage over that rope Jean-Paul left out."

Her brows knit. "Oh, you saw me? I thought you were

asleep." She smiled into his chest, the movement of her lips tickling the hair there.

He smiled too and held her closer, content to sit with this tiny, perfect woman in his arms. "You owe me a nap," he said.

"How can a person owe a nap?"

"I'd just settled in for one when you showed up. I haven't been able to sleep without you in my arms since."

"You slept that first night in your cabin."

"No sleep. I tossed and turned."

The smile on her face was pure female satisfaction.

10

"Take the free end up through the eye, around the standing part and back where it came from." Jared watched as Teri's tongue came out as she concentrated. The things she could do with that tongue amazed him. "There, you did it. A perfect bowline knot. It'll never slip or jam if you make it right."

He grinned at her, pleased she was such a willing student. Willing to learn and competent enough to follow through on her own. The past five days had been incredible.

They were dressed in swimsuits this morning because a sixty-footer had joined them in the cove at sunset the night before. The *Sally-Rose* dwarfed the *SandJack*.

Jared couldn't take his eyes off her. "She's got great lines," he said.

"She's very pretty. I like the maroon awnings." Teri stretched out on a lounge chair with a bowl of fruit and yogurt for breakfast. He'd watched her dip slices of melon into the yogurt and lick the creamy stuff off with that mischievous tongue until he wanted to dash the bowl to the deck and take her mouth.

They'd hailed the *Sally-Rose* the night before and spoken to the captain, a newcomer to the Caribbean.

The yacht was for sale and an old urge had come to life as soon as he'd heard. Since leaving the rat race, he'd been content to drift for months at a time, living easy.

But his bent for profit-and-loss statements had kicked in at first sight of the yacht.

"What's going through your mind? You're distracted this morning," Teri said, with a shift of her legs on the lounge chair. He grinned, smoothed a palm from her knee to her groin.

"Don't try to change the subject," she said tartly. "I see you eying the *Sally-Rose* with the same kind of lust you've had for me. What's up?"

"The honeymoon charter idea for the *SandJack* took off like gangbusters. Now that I've got a Web site, I've got charters booked solid."

Her eyes flared interest and she leaned forward at attention. She set her fruit aside. "But you could do more with the *Sally-Rose*. Corporate stuff. Bigger events."

"Exactly." Their eyes met in mutual understanding. He could see her mind skipping around, turned on by something other than sex.

And that turned him on.

"You know how some corporations send teams out to the wilderness for camps to develop team spirit?"

"You make me so hot," he blurted, as crazy for the way her mind worked as he was for her tight little rocket of a body. "We could take them diving."

"Or to swim with sharks."

"And there's cave diving."

"Isn't that really dangerous?"

"And swimming with sharks isn't?"

She laughed, then sobered. "You said 'we.'"

"What?" But his mind was racing with possibilities and he

was even happier to know she understood, that her mind was in synch with his.

"Never mind," she said. "Come here and kiss me."

"I like when you're bossy." He picked her up off the lounge chair and kissed her deeply. The spark between them snapped harder than ever, but they both welcomed it now, knowing the only thing to mellow it was deep touching.

For the rest of the early morning Jared taught her more knots. Then they killed another hour by taking a swim off the swim grid.

The *Sally-Rose* seemed slow to come to life but eventually, they saw signs that the crew was awake and preparing to weigh anchor. Jared nodded toward the yacht, one hand grasping the rail of the swim grid. "They'll be gone soon. I was going to suggest we head out to sea, but now that they're leaving we can stay here if you'd like."

"I'd like. There's no need to go anywhere else. I have everything I want and need right here."

They climbed aboard and dried off, then stretched out to cover each other with sunblock. Long teasing drizzles of lotion led to long teasing kisses.

Jared carried her below and stretched out under her on the leather sofa. No longer afraid of hurting her with his size, he delighted in lifting Teri to straddle him. He pumped into her like a piston. It was fast, hard and immediate.

She was always ready, always wet, always welcoming.

Her small hands dug into his pecs, her nails grazing him as she worked his cock. Her breasts bounced, her pussy slid in maddening circles around his stiff pole as she did figure eights on his lap. Her tongue came out as she got close and when she came her mouth opened on a guttural cry. She exploded around his cock, her inner walls contracting and squeezing him. He spurted deep into her, taken over the edge of sanity.

"I love it that you like it fast."

She fell to his chest, curled her fingers around his head and nodded. "Yes, I love it fast. I love it slow. I love it with you."

He pulled his head back to try to see her face, but her eyes closed on a sated sigh. He kissed the tip of her nose and bit back what he wanted to say.

After they showered he went back up on deck to see if the yacht had left yet, but the *Sally-Rose* was still in the cove. He considered her carefully. With a salon and three bedrooms and room for a small crew, she'd make a great complement to the *SandJack*.

While the *SandJack* was perfect for the kind of intimacy he enjoyed with Teri, the *Sally-Rose* could handle larger parties.

Jared extended an awning for shade and set up a board game. He had already lost several times to Teri's better skill at a cross-word game.

For payback, he planned to beat her into the ground on real estate. He set up the game's bank and counted out their share of money to start the game while she brought up a batch of choco-late chip cookies. If the snap and crackle between them wasn't enough to make him love her, then her habit of baking for fun and relaxation would.

The unique womanly scent of Teri drifted past his nose. She smelled of soap and fresh salty air and chocolate. She aimed a chocolate chip cookie at his mouth. He bit it, chewed slowly, savoring the still-warm flavor. "These are fantastic." He licked his lips to get all the chocolate flavor.

She grinned. "I'm glad you like them. You look like a little boy when you do that. Makes me see the hellion you must have been."

"I believe I heard that word a time or two. But only when my mom didn't know I was in earshot and always spoken under her breath."

The game began and Jared focused intently, surprised at the

competitive edge he brought to the game. He hadn't felt this way in a couple years, but he couldn't help himself.

Finally, the *Sally-Rose* weighed anchor and they stood to wave them off. When they sat down again, she laughed. "Whose roll is it?"

"Mine."

"Why is it always your turn when we forget?"

"It's my game." His stash of board games had caught her eye earlier that morning when she'd gone looking in the storage bunks under the sofas for cookie sheets. He rolled a six and moved his game piece. "Aha! I get to buy this to complete my set. I want to put a house on the property."

"Showoff." She laughed and passed him a plastic house.

He looked at it closely. "Look, there's a door and windows."

"Most houses have them."

"And a yard, with kids and a dog," he said when he set it down on his square of property. He raised an eyebrow at her. "Did you want that?"

"Not last week. Last week I wanted a bigger Manhattan apartment with dreams of a nice co-op in my future. In white, of course, with a splash of ivory for color." She mimicked a voice he could only think was Philip's.

She looked wistful. "But now, maybe a house will come along some day. And kids, too."

"And your promotion?"

"Will hopefully lead to more. But the market's tough. It can break people stronger than me."

"Going back to that kind of pressure turns your crank?"

She frowned. "Of course." Her frown deepened. "Maybe."

He let her stew a moment and she continued to think.

"I'm not sure I know how to answer. Why do you ask?"

"I've been there. Did the whole corporate ladder climb and walked away."

"Why?"

"So I could play sea captain and take naps." He picked up the die. "My turn."

"Anyone who looked at the *Sally-Rose* with the kind of lust I saw in your eyes this morning is way beyond playing sea captain and taking naps. No, you're more ambitious than that."

"I'd need a first mate, someone I could depend on. A partner."

"Anyone come to mind?"

He had to look away in case she saw the way his mind had turned. He had to be careful, let her come to her own conclusion. Forcing the issue might frighten her off. "It's my turn to roll."

"No, it isn't. It's mine." She reached to take the die from his hand. He snagged her wrist and pulled her close. Her smiling face came within kissing range so kiss her he did, putting an end to the conversation. She didn't need to hear why he'd packed it in, but she sure as hell needed to think about why she should.

And this kiss was only one of many reasons.

11

Teri wasn't fooled by the kiss. Jared wanted to change the subject. She was tempted to let him think he'd gotten away with it, but the competitive spirit she'd nurtured in her career climb wouldn't let her. She pulled out of his arms. "Not so fast, lover boy. What happened? How did you end up on the *SandJack*?"

"I'm not going to whine about my divorce. We were not compatible. Our life goals changed after awhile."

She glanced around at the thirty-five feet of absurd luxury. "What, did she want to live in a regular house with you at a regular job?"

"Being in a marriage should mean being able to be yourself. Compromise is important, but it's a two-way street. She couldn't handle that I wanted more freedom." He opened his arms to indicate the boat. "She was after the big house, the high-end cars, all the stuff I used to think I wanted. When I changed my mind, she left." Jared looked out across the bay toward the open water, following the wake of the *Sally-Rose* for a moment in silence.

He tugged Teri onto her back, and she went willingly. Denying Jared anything was hard to do. She craved his touch far more than she could have imagined. The electricity between them seduced her as much as the man himself. The hum of it, the stroke of heat that sizzled to her loins was a drug she was beginning to think she couldn't live without.

She ignored the warnings she heard from her heart and stretched out beneath him, forgetting the board game, forgetting her life in New York, forgetting everything but this man and this moment. The weight of him was welcome, the touch of his skin was welcome, the nuzzling mouth at her neck did marvelous things right through her body. She couldn't deny him a thing.

"I can think of a million different things we could talk about instead," he said.

"Like what?" she said through a smile. She wrapped her arms around his neck and reached up to kiss him quickly.

"Like where on your body I could hide some chocolate chips." He nuzzled her ear, breathing heavily and tickling her with his beard stubble.

She screeched with laughter. "Where? Where?"

"I'll show you, my pretty, arrr." He put on the voice of a wolfish marauder. His eyes lit with wild lust, intent and focused on her. "You'll just have to wait while I go get them."

He ran down the hatch to get the bag of chocolate chips. She had all of ten seconds to hide, so with a screech of laughter, she leaped to her feet, took off to the far side of the hot tub and crouched there, balancing on the balls of her feet.

She clamped a hand over her mouth to stop the sound of her giggles from reaching him. He reappeared at the hatch, stood and shook the bag in his fist over his head, rattling it like a saber.

Teri rolled her eyes. But a thrill rose through her belly at the idea of being chased, caught and at his mercy.

His head turned from side to side slowly as he pretended to growl with a menace that held an underlying tone of humor.

She heard him clear his throat and had to suppress more giggles. Feeling like a playful child, she undid her bra and tossed it across the deck to land on the back of a deck chair.

The pirate turned and picked up the scrap of cloth. Sniffed it. Growled louder. When he went into a hunter's crouch she nearly lost it.

If it hadn't been for the knuckles she wedged into her mouth, she'd have been rolling on the deck in a fit of laughter.

The man was ridiculous fun and it warmed her heart to see the clown he could be.

Some of the noise she was trying to stifle must have reached him, because his gaze zeroed in on the hot tub and he took a menacing step toward her.

With a screech, she bounded from the cover of the hot tub and made a dash for the bow. A loud war whoop goosed her to run faster.

Panting for breath, she turned and faced the ravisher, her breasts swinging, feet spread, hair flying in the breeze.

Jared stopped dead, the bag forgotten in his hand. "You are so beautiful," he said, his voice reverent, all play gone.

She dropped her sarong to the deck and took off, blushing with the realization that he truly felt in his heart that she was beautiful.

He chased her with the bag of chips, growling menacingly again. She dodged around the whole boat, leaving her thong on the wheel. He followed the trail of clothing and laughter, giving her plenty of time to step out of reach.

When she decided to let him catch her, they were both out of breath, but he still held the bag of chips.

And she was deliciously naked. He drew her down to one of the upholstered benches.

"Oooh, Mr. Pirate, you're so big and strong, I don't know how to fight you off."

She squirmed under his hands, lighting the fire of his arousal.

He sprinkled five of the small chocolate buds on her belly and licked them off, one by one. Each swipe of his tongue sent fire to her deepest parts and she quieted a little more until she lay stretched out, waiting for whatever delicious torture he would apply next.

Slick with desire, her pussy open, her clit needy, she was ready when he finally dragged her legs up against his chest and looped her knees over his shoulders. Slowly, one by one he dropped chocolates onto her dewy crotch.

Bending to her he found each softening bit of chocolate with his mouth. He sucked each one up, licking her inner lips each time. Her breathing changed, became more shallow and rapid with each flick of his tongue. Tension built, but still he took his time, pretending more interest in the chocolate than in her. He swirled her clit, sucking it firmly between his lips. She arched, lifting her ass into the air in a futile bid to have him take her over the edge.

The pirate was driving her mad with need. Finally, he slid his tongue into her crevice, letting her juices pool and slide between her ass cheeks to drip on the bunk. She'd never been so turned on, so wet.

His eyes gleamed in a way that spoke of even more delights. He followed the line of her juice, lapping at her while he plunged two wide blunt fingers into her channel. Her inner walls rejoiced with the filling.

Finally, finally he was going to give her what she craved.

"Yes, do it! Take me there!"

She felt his mouth on her again, his tongue dancing on her dewy clit as she came in a wild burst of moisture that drenched his hand and face.

When the final pulses died away, Jared turned her to kneel, her hands braced on the deck railing and took her from behind. In a gesture meant to torture her captor, she reached between her legs and clasped his balls as they swung against her with each plunge.

His cry was instant and she felt the inner gush from his come fill her. His fingers found her again and with a ravenous focus there was no holding back. Jared took everything she had to give and more. Wrenching every last element of satisfaction from her, she was limp by the end, unable to stand.

"You are incredible," she said drowsily. "This whole time is incredible and I'll never forget it. I would show you my appreciation, but I can't move."

"If you really want to show your appreciation, bake more cookies."

"Hm, how do you feel about pie?" The feeling was beginning to return to her legs.

"Key lime?"

She grinned. "As soon as I can stand, I'll bake you a key lime pie."

"I think I love you," he said, lightheartedly.

"Keep making love to me this way and I'll begin to believe it," she responded in kind. Rolling to her feet, she padded off toward the galley. "Next time," she called back over her shoulder, "we do it in bed. My back can't take the hard deck anymore."

The days continued in a wild spree of champagne and great sex and loving afterglow. Jared was attentive, patient and made Teri feel pampered. He treated her like a perfect lady, a perfect lover and a perfect partner. He taught her how to tie more knots, how to pilot the boat, how to weigh anchor and how to make love. He showed her how it could be between two people who respected and truly liked each other. She had never come close to this kind of relationship before in her life.

Her family had been warm enough, but suffocating in their

concern. She had hurt them when she left for New York, claiming she was going to get a high-powered job, make a grand success of her life and leave behind the mousy girl they'd raised.

Five years later, she'd done it all. And until recently, she'd felt pretty good about how her life had turned out, but now she was wondering if her success was worth the price.

Half the time she was worried about weight gain, most of the time she was worried about her career, and until Philip had called a halt to their sex life, sex had become an item on her "to do" list. She'd even stopped baking, something that came as natural to her as breathing.

And the wedding had taken on the proportions of a monster threatening to eat Manhattan.

But here, with Jared, none of that mattered. For these few days, she was free, and unconditionally accepted. The sex was intense, fun and experimental. She reveled in the freedom Jared gave her.

Even Teri realized she was blossoming into a freedom-loving hedonist, a part of her personality she had always kept under wraps. Knowing these same days spent with her ex would never have produced these changes, she blossomed. She hadn't laughed this much in all the time she'd been with Philip.

On her last morning, Teri woke, and lay curled on her side, facing Jared. The deep, even breathing she heard reassured and comforted her, while creating a sharp dread. *Not yet! Don't think about it.*

She snuggled close and rested her head on his furred chest and drank in his early morning scent. Musky, with the leftover scent of wild loving, it made her hot.

Sliding down the warm length of him, Teri found his resting cock and coaxed it to life with her mouth. Jared's breathing changed and she knew he was awake as the blood rushed to fill the hot flesh in her mouth. She felt his fingers in her hair and

the tug that indicated he wanted to slide inside her, but she refused to leave her position.

She wanted to take him over the edge this way. Wanted to
give to him unselfishly, so he'd never forget the touch of her
mouth and this last morning together.

She took him quick and hard, laving him, increasing the tension, the suction and the dance of her fingers across his sac. He
exploded in her mouth in a wild buck that pleased her with its
suddenness. She'd learned so much about pleasure, so much
about pleasing a man, so much about pleasing herself.

Indeed, Teri Branton was a new woman, returning to a
brand new life.

She slid up to wrap her arms around his chest. "Thank you
for this week, Jared. I can't tell you how different I feel. Better,
stronger, more alive."

"So do I. You've changed me, too."

She smiled, pleased. "How much longer do we have?"

"A couple of hours. Normally, I'd have docked in Kingston
last night, but I can squeeze my prep time into the afternoon.
My next charter clients arrive at four."

She felt his seeking hand travel south of her waist. She
opened her legs, well past the shyness of early acquaintance.
"When does your flight leave?" he asked as he slid his fingers
into her slickness.

"Tonight." She arched as his fingers plunged, as quick and
hard as she'd been with him. He'd always been more gentle
than this, but the speed and aggression thrilled her. She responded with a slide of moisture. He made her so hot!

He plunged and retreated several times, quick, quick, hard,
bringing her to a tension-filled peak faster than ever before.
"I'm ready," she murmured. "Now!"

But he slid to cover her. "Not yet, I have to be inside, have
to feel you as you clench and come."

The solid weight of him pressed on her and she sighed with

the rightness of it. She ran her hands down his back, folding her legs around his, tucking into him. Feeling the head of his cock at her entrance, she pushed up, opening fully and closing around him. She was full of Jared one last time.

She rocked against him, nipped at his ear, licked the salt from his neck and drank in the scent of fully aroused male. Taken back to primal time, they danced the dance of man and woman.

When Jared strained against her, she felt his pulsing cock and rushed headlong into her own climax, as he bucked into her.

He settled against her neck, cradling her in his arms, and she spoke. "I don't know what you've done to me, but I can promise you, I'll never be the same again," she murmured.

He chuckled and she grinned into his chest. Her legs were boneless as she sprawled on the bed. He kissed the tip of her nose and whispered into her ear. "Stay for another week."

12

The invitation stunned Teri. Touched by his coaxing tone, she hated to refuse him. "I can't stay another week. I have to get back to work." The words popped out without thought. Of course she had to return to her life. She had a job, a career, a promotion waiting.

Everything she'd worked for was within reach.

And she had the stilettos to prove it.

Jared pulled away, sat on the edge of the bed, his back to her. His magnificent, broad-shouldered, slim-waisted, muscular back. He'd never looked so forbidding.

"It's very sweet of you to ask me. I appreciate it. Maybe I can come back for my next vacation?"

"Sure, that's what you'll do. Come back another time." He stood and headed toward the shower. Like the first morning she'd seen him tousled from bed, he stretched and reached for the ceiling.

She catalogued the memory of this, too.

She tried to imagine him in her apartment stretching in the morning. Even he wouldn't be able to touch the ceiling there.

She was at a loss. This was not supposed to happen. She thought about her next vacation. She was not supposed to feel this wild excitement at the prospect of seeing him again.

Seeing him, Jared. Her pirate. She tried to place him in Manhattan. Maybe sitting in a theater, laughing with her at a musical comedy.

No, that didn't fit. If he visited New York he'd be at the docks.

Tears built behind her eyes, but she refused to let them fall. Simple visits wouldn't be enough to sustain what they shared and she knew it.

She owed Jared so much, but there were no words. She heard the shower running and considered joining him, but the stall was too small for two, even two connected at the hips.

She had to go back to her own life. She had wedding presents to return, and she needed to make arrangements to stay in her apartment. By now, it would be all over the studio that she'd been left at the altar. She dreaded the questions and the pitying looks, but she could handle them. She had to prove she was okay, had to face everyone.

She'd get back to work, throw herself into landing that promotion and show everyone she was fine. In fighting spirit.

For Thanksgiving, she'd go to Kansas to be with her family just like usual. She thought about four days on the *SandJack* instead. Decided it would be too hard to be here again. Four days wouldn't be enough.

Not nearly enough.

She would do whatever she could to keep thoughts of Jared at bay. Work hard, play hard, take up jogging, work longer hours, harder hours. Whatever it took, she'd do it until this time on the *SandJack* became just a gentle memory with no power to hurt.

It was sweet that he'd asked her to stay longer, but another week of this and she feared she wouldn't want to leave. And that was definitely not what Jared wanted. No, he wanted his freedom. He'd made that plain when he'd spoken of his divorce and his wife's demands.

Jared let the hot water sluice down his sex-ravaged body. Teri wore him out, beat him at all his board games, sent his taste buds to heaven with her baking and made him laugh. Knowing she was leaving was killing him.

He'd led the conversations as much as he'd dared. He'd tried to get her to think about her life in New York, that maybe things had changed now, but she was as stubborn blind as she was hot.

He'd even asked her to stay another week and been refused. If he tried to explain about the sparks and love at first touch and the men in his family, she'd say he was crazy. He probably was.

Well, shit. If he was crazy, then every MacKay male that ever lived was, too. Could this kind of crazy be hereditary?

He scrubbed his chest and his scalp to clear his thoughts. Teri could keep him befuddled with sex. The more he had the more he wanted.

He wanted her, but she'd given no indication her feelings went deeper than having a good time for a short time. She'd even laughed at his suggestion she stay for another week. Totally focused on returning to work, she'd missed the urgency in his voice when he'd issued the invitation.

He had charters booked through the next three months and he couldn't afford to cancel any, not when the business had just started to take off. He didn't have anyone he could trust with his clients, so leaving to go to New York with her for a while was out of the question.

Not that he'd been invited.

He went to the galley to make coffee the way Teri liked it and couldn't come up with anything to convince her to stay but the bald truth. He was in love and wanted to marry her.

But on a week's worth of sex and vacation time, she'd never believe it.

Later that morning, the *SandJack* slipped easily into her place on the pier, and Teri scrambled to secure the bow, while Jared took care of the stern.

He knew she was looking for some kind of formal good-bye, some special words between them. But he couldn't think of one right thing to say. There weren't any words that would suffice for him.

He wasn't the kind of man who said, "Thanks, Teri, you were great," as if grading her performance. And time had already run out. Usually, he returned to dock in the wee hours of the morning so he would have time to restock the food and liquor, but he'd broken his own rule to have a couple more hours with her.

Now he barely had enough time to get the linens and food delivered and his cleaning crew aboard.

Jared seemed distracted by all the details of settling the *SandJack* into her berth, so Teri headed into the cabin to get her luggage, ducking her face so Jared wouldn't see how distressed she was.

What was the point in letting him know she didn't want to leave? These days had been a brief, frivolous time carved out of an unfrivolous life. Of course, she wouldn't want to leave, she told herself. Who would?

But she was an adult now, not the grown-up girl who had waited at the altar for words that never came. Jared had turned her into a woman willing to live her life on her own terms and she would be forever grateful.

But that didn't mean he wanted her here forever. No, this whole thing belonged in the mists of memory and that's exactly where she was going to file it. It would soon be nothing more than a pleasant thought, a quiet smile, an errant scent on the breeze.

She thought he might follow her into the cabin to help with the suitcases, but he didn't come. It was better this way. There would be no time for private good-byes. They'd done that before breakfast, and after. Then again, one last time, in the tiny shower with Jared buried so deep she was barely able to roll her hips. They came with next to no movement, eye to eye, letting their minds and hearts bring them to the pinnacle. She'd shattered in his arms, feet, elbows and knees braced against the tight, slick shower walls, pinioned in place.

She hoisted her luggage and dragged the larger suitcases up to the deck. Then she went after her carry-on bag. The points of her stiletto heels still jutted, threatening to poke holes in the bag.

She unzipped it and dug the shoes out. This pair was black, nearly new. She recalled watching her wedding shoes fill with water and sink into oblivion. Dread filled her chest at the idea of putting these shoes back on.

Once she did, she really would be off the *SandJack* and on her way back home. She picked them up, letting them dangle from two fingers, grabbed her bag and headed up the hatchway to the deck without looking back.

Jared waited on the deck to help her disembark. His expression was all business. Even cheery, she thought. Was he glad she was leaving?

She bit her lip so she wouldn't ask. She liked him too much to put him on the spot that way. No, it would be far better to walk away and smile all the way to the airport.

He lifted her suitcases onto the wooden planks of the dock.

The glance he gave her was cursory, moved from the top of her head to her feet. "No shoes?"

She appreciated his tone. Soft, easy and natural. Like the man himself. "Not on board," she said.

She lifted her hand, the stilettos dangling.

He noted them, his eyes hard and flinty.

She hoped for a quick peck on the cheek, maybe even a warm hug, but found him looking toward a couple who were quickly advancing toward the *SandJack*. They looked flushed, happy and excited.

They looked the way honeymooners should look. "Damn, they're early," he said.

She turned away and climbed onto the dock quickly, not wanting an awkward parting. Jared didn't have to help her, she'd become much more agile and sure-footed during her stay.

The other couple neared and she heard them exclaim. "Look at that boat!"

She raised her head to see what they were talking about.

The *Sally-Rose* was moored a couple hundred yards off-shore. She glanced at Jared at the same time he looked at her.

His eyes were hard, searching.

She dropped her stilettos to the dock.

"Yes," he said to the couple, "I'm thinking of putting an offer in on her. She's a beauty."

Teri's heart stalled. She looked at her shoes, one upright the other lying on its side. She straightened it, preparing to put them on.

The other couple jostled past her in their excitement to climb aboard. She felt at sea, adrift, bereft of the comfort of Jared. She bit her lip, trying not to cry.

She waited a moment, not knowing what it was she waited for.

Jared MacKay was the captain of the *SandJack*, ready and

willing to give his customers everything they needed for a romantic getaway.

Which was exactly what Teri had had. *Be an adult, put on your shoes and walk away.*

She lifted her right foot and slid it into the shoe. She rose on the teetering heel.

"The problem with the *Sally-Rose* is, she's too big to sail alone. I'd need a first mate," he said, his voice carrying clearly.

Teri slid her second shoe on. Her toes protested and her insteps felt stretched by the high arches. Jared's voice came again, and through a swim of tears, she looked at him.

"But if I were to have a first mate, she'd have to know how to bake."

Teri blinked and the watery image of Jared leaping the deck railing to the dock made her shudder. Blindly she held her arms out to him and felt him sweep her up into a hard embrace. Her feet dangled as he turned her face up to his and drowned her in a kiss.

When he lifted his head he whispered, "Those high heels are going to have to come off, ma'am."

"I'll never wear them again." She toed one then the other to the dock. Jared kicked them into the sea. "This first mate," she said, "could she use her contacts in the TV and movie industry to help build your charter business?"

The hum of electricity they shared zapped from one to the other and settled in their hearts.

"Hm, sounds a lot more like a partner than a first mate." He nuzzled her neck, setting her skin afire.

She grinned, happier in this golden moment than she'd ever been before. "I love you, my pirate."

"Be my wife, Teri. Share my life and we'll be free together. I love you."

She slid to her feet and copied Jared's leap over the railing onto the deck of the *SandJack*, thirty-five feet of decadent luxury filled with intimacy, love and honeymoon joy.

Bonnie Edwards is happy to hear from readers through her Web site at www.bonnieedwards.com *where news, covers and updates are posted regularly.*

THE CRIB

SASHA WHITE

1

A heady mixture of adrenaline and arousal coursed through my veins as I lifted the half-full snifter to my lips to sip at the creamy concoction. I'd been trying for hours to wrap my mind around the latest news I'd received. Jimmy D, a man I considered family, was a murder suspect. My temper had been simmering since I got off the phone, and I couldn't seem to get a grip.

I'd learned that the only way for me to deal when that happened was to go in search of a physical release. A fight was one way to take the edge off my emotions and give me a chance to think again, but my sparring partner was out of town, so I had gone with option two.

Setting the drink down again, I swiped my tongue slowly across my top lip to catch anything left behind, and watched my companion's eyes darken. A slow flush crept across his high cheekbones and he inched closer.

He was a good-looking guy. In a clean-cut, boy-next-door kind of way that made him look younger than he probably was. Not my usual type. However, I knew for a fact that looks could be deceiving. And the fact that he was hanging out in this bar, a

known meat market, told me that he wasn't as naïve or innocent as he appeared.

Just like I wasn't as frail or delicate as I appeared.

"What was your name again?" I tossed my hair over my
shoulder and looked him up and down.

"Steve," he answered.

"Are you horny, Steve?"

Now it was his neck that slowly turned red. I slipped my
hand below the edge of the bar, leaned into him, and reaching
between his legs, tested his size. His cock swelled beneath my
fingers, and a satisfying feeling of power swept over me.

Men. They were so predictable.

"I think you've discovered the answer to that question
yourself," he spoke with confidence.

With a naughty smile I stroked him a few times through his
trousers. That was all it took. He reached into his pocket and
tossed a few bills on the bar for the tab. Stepping back, he took
my now empty hand in his, and we exited the bar.

The night air was humid and the parking lot was dark, a
couple of the lights along the roof of the building burned out. I
automatically scanned my surroundings, noticing dark corners
and the proximity of potential danger zones. It was the perfect
place for illicit activities.

God, I loved the rush of living on the edge, of doing the un-
expected.

Steve lead the way across the parking lot, with me following
him, not saying a word. Instead, I focused on the way my heart
raced, my pussy lips plumped, and my juices pooled between
my thighs.

He hadn't even touched me yet. The overeager reaction of
my body was a clear sign I was doing the right thing. I needed
this liberation from my tangled thoughts for just a short time.

Steve stopped next to a big, shiny red pickup truck that was
backed up against the building, and beeped the door unlocked.

"This is yours?"

"Yup." He ushered me between the truck and the compact car parked next to it. "Where are you going?"

Instead of climbing into the truck like he'd expected, I continued to walk toward the building. With a quick glance I confirmed my suspicions. There was just enough room for what I had in mind.

Reaching into my bra I skipped over the small blade I kept nestled between my breasts, and pulled out the condom I'd tucked next to it earlier. I handed it to Steve, and then let down the tailgate of the truck.

Bending over the end of the truck, I planted my hands on the truck bed and spread my legs, feeling the cool air on my hot sex. I looked over my shoulder, quirked an eyebrow at the gaping man, and wiggled my tail.

"Here?" he croaked.

"Here."

An eager grin spread across his expressive face and he couldn't unzip his pants fast enough. Once I saw him rolling the condom onto his rigid hard-on, I turned away and looked out over the parking lot.

"Lexy, baby," he said as he lifted my skirt and grabbed my hips. "You're a fantasy come to life, aren't you?"

"Don't talk, Steve." I arched my back and thrust back against his groin. Reaching between my legs with one hand I gripped his cock, guiding him to my entrance. "You'll ruin the fantasy."

An ecstatic groan echoed in the empty lot as he thrust deep. My eyelids dropped to half-mast and I fought to keep my head up, to keep my eyes on the other dark corners as my insides pulsed low and heavy. The thrill of the forbidden enhanced the fire burning through my veins. A moan slipped from me when the man behind me gripped my hips tighter, and pumped into me faster and harder. His rigid cock slid in and out, filling me and pulling away in delicious torture. Our panting breaths filled the silence in the dark night air and my insides started to clench. A mini spasm swept over me when I caught movement out of the corner of my eye.

It was another couple, strolling into the parking lot, arms wrapped around each other. They hadn't seen us yet and I doubted they would as they were heading for the other side of the lot. But just the chance that we might get caught had me striving for the orgasm already building inside me. I lifted a hand from the truck bed, reached between my thighs, and pinched my swollen clit.

A shudder racked my body, and I bit my lip to stifle my outcry as pleasure rolled over me in waves. My orgasm set off Steve's and he bucked against me, groaning loud enough for the couple across the parking lot to turn in our direction before jumping into their car quickly.

Steve leaned over my back for a few seconds to catch his breath before pulling out. I used that time to catch my own breath and shake off any misplaced sense of shame.

I turned to Steve after pulling my skirt down, and patted him on the cheek softly. "Thanks. I needed that."

"Can I get your number?" he called out as I walked away.

I didn't bother to answer. The orgasm had cleared my head, and I knew what I had to do. I didn't really want to go back to Edmonton, but I wasn't about to stand by and lose another loved one when I could do something about it.

Most men think women use sex to get what they want, out of them, out of life. But I know different. I know that women are trained from childhood to believe that sex is something special, to be shared only with someone special. That it's more than just an urge, or a natural high. I know that if women really used sex as a weapon, they'd be more dangerous.

They'd be more like me.

2

I needed more information, and I needed it fast. As a private investigator, with skip tracing as a sideline, getting information from the unwilling was a talent I'd developed over the years.

Leaning low over the scarred oak bar, I wiped at the already clean draft taps, wiggling along with the John Cougar Mellencamp classic playing on the jukebox. The Crib was a small bar in an old neighborhood of Edmonton. The usual clientele was mostly blue-collar workers; bikers, truckers, mechanics, and a few students from the nearby community college.

My little dance moves flashed the three guys sitting at the bar nursing their beers a good deal of cleavage. And that was okay, because if I was going to catch the killer, I needed to know what these guys knew. I wasn't after just any killer, but *the* killer. The one that was willing to let Jimmy D, the owner of The Crib, an establishment I'd spent my teen years running rampant in, pay for a crime he didn't commit.

Jimmy was my Uncle Tony's best friend, my first love's father, and a man who would forever be close to my heart. When I'd first heard from my uncle that Jimmy was in trouble, I'd struggled with a boatload of emotions, some of which had been buried deep for years.

The guilt of not being there for Jimmy when he needed me brought back the childhood guilt that I was off at a friend's house, enjoying a sleepover while my parents were getting killed in a B & E gone bad. Then there was the fury I'd buried when their killers went free on a technicality.

My Uncle Tony took me on to raise, and Jimmy D had become an honorary uncle. The Crib had been as much a home as Tony's Bike Shop. The thought that the very system that had failed to punish my parents' killers was now trying to take away another family member had put me into a tailspin, and landed me back in my old hometown after ten years away without a visit.

Some mindless action in a dark parking lot had helped me get my emotions back under control and I was ready to work the case. Someone needed to make sure the cops didn't lock up the wrong guy, and I'd decided that someone would be me. I didn't trust anyone else. That's how I ended up posing as a cocktail waitress in Jimmy's bar.

It was a quiet night, and the place was almost empty. Unfortunately, that's the way it had been since I showed up back in town the day after Jimmy's "visit" at the cop shop. That was ten days ago. They'd pulled him in for questioning two times since, but they'd yet to actually arrest him, or anyone else.

You'd think that the owner of a biker bar getting questioned for murder wouldn't hurt his business. But it had. A local junkie gets stabbed in the back alley, and business suffers. Even that of a roughneck bar.

The realization that even if Jimmy didn't go to jail, he could lose his business, made me antsy to kick up the search.

"So guys, where's the party?" I pasted a flirty smile on my face and asked the guys parked on the stools in front of me.

"What party is that?"

All three of them were dressed in a combination of leather jackets, vests, and denim jeans. They all had visible tattoos, and one of them desperately needed a shower and shave. I could smell him from five feet away.

Unfortunately, it was he who answered me.

With two steps I was directly in front of him, elbows rested on the bar, giving off the naughty girl vibes I knew would make him think he had a chance at getting lucky. He wasn't bad looking, but the scent was a huge turnoff.

"The one where I can get my hands on some treats. I've only been in town for a week or so, and I haven't had a chance to make any connections yet." I spoke softly and ran a fingertip over the hand that cupped his beer between us. I tried not to cringe at the ragged and dirty fingernails, and arched an eyebrow at him suggestively. "You know what I mean?"

"Yeah, I know what you mean, baby. But there's no party tonight, just a bike show." He eyed me hungrily. "I really wish I could help you out. Why don't you give me your number and if I hear of any *parties* going down I'll give you a call?"

I'd learned early on in life that the sight of a nice pair of breasts jiggling in front of their face made most men stupid, or at the very least, sloppy. I checked my gut and it told me this guy wasn't lying. It also urged me to give him a way to contact me because he might know more than he was saying.

"Sure," I said, and wrote my cell phone number on the back of a cardboard coaster for him.

He told me his name was Tim, and that he'd see what he could do for me. Before he could try and get any friendlier, I moved to the other end of the bar and wondered if the night was going to be a complete loss. Giving Tim my number might pay off eventually, but it probably wasn't going to be soon.

Gazing out onto the floor of the bar I searched for another possible source of information. The well-worn pool tables in the back of the bar looked forlorn, and the square tables that filled the floor between them and the bar sat empty in the middle of the room. Two of the cushioned booths that lined the walls were occupied; one housed a college student set up with books spread out in front of him and a jug of beer close at hand, and another with a couple arguing. Neither of them pulled at me.

If I was really just a cocktail waitress I'd probably enjoy the downtime. After all, waitressing was hard work. But as a woman on a mission, I was bored and frustrated with the lack of action. How the hell was I supposed to figure out who the bad guy was if he didn't come into the bar?

I knew the killer would come back. I'd managed to wiggle some details of the case from a local cop when I'd arrived in town. From what he said, someone had been dealing out the back door of The Crib for more than a year now, and the junk he was selling was getting increasingly bad. It wasn't just pot, the cops had traced a few batches of crystal meth back to the bar, as well as some heroin. They figured that even if Jimmy wasn't the one actually selling it, he was in charge of what was going on.

I knew Jimmy would never be into something like that, so that meant the connection was either staff, or a regular. Jimmy swore the cops were barking up the wrong tree, that none of his staff would deal drugs out of his bar. But as much as I disliked cops, I knew that if they were on that trail, they had to have a reason for it.

Anger bubbled inside me. The Crib had been around for almost thirty years. A miracle in this business, but the place stayed alive because Jimmy treated his staff fairly, and his regulars like family, at the very least like friends. It boggled my mind to believe a *friend* could be responsible, but that was the way it looked.

The whole point of me coming back to town and slinging beer was to clear Jimmy's name. With his history, I knew he was innocent. Well, innocent of dealing drugs and murdering a buyer anyway. If it were a dealer who had been found dead, and not the buyer, I'd be more inclined to believe he'd done it.

Nobody peddles shit in The Crib without Jimmy coming down on him. Hard. And everybody knew why.

"Lexy, sweetheart, can I have another beer down here?"

Not willing to take *that* trip down memory lane at the moment, I was glad for the distraction of serving some drinks.

Stinky Tim got up from the bar, gathered his things and waved good-bye as I filled a frosty glass with draft. When it was foaming over I strolled down the bar with hips swinging, to Bear. Placing the mug in front of the big guy I winked flirtatiously. "Anything else I can do for you?"

"Sure, honey," he said with a loopy grin. "I could use a tongue bath."

"That wasn't what I had in mind, Bear. But if you insist, I know just the girl to give it to you." Letting myself relax a bit, I strolled out from behind the bar to stand next to him, pursed my lips and let out a sharp whistle. "Daisy!"

Loud guffaws and chuckles echoed in the near empty room when Jimmy's rottweiler bitch came trotting out of his office to sit by my feet. She looked up at me adoringly; pink tongue lolling out from between gleaming canine teeth.

"Hey! No need to get nasty. You asked if there was anything else you could do for me!" Bear chuckled good-naturedly.

Scratching Daisy's head absentmindedly I listened as the two guys on the left tossed playful insults back and forth. Never one to stay away from her man for long, Daisy soon headed back to the office, and I leaned against the bar and joked with them to help time pass.

Basically good men, but of the rough and raw category, I'd just finished telling them a dirty joke when the doors swung open and a group streamed in. I didn't pay them much mind, until I saw *him*.

My body temperature jumped and the air crackled with energy. Tall, dark, and dangerous-looking, he was pure sin. And I wanted him from the first second I'd laid eyes on him.

There was just something about him that called to me. He'd been in the bar a couple of times in the last week, but it never failed that when I started my shift, he was on his way out the door.

Seems my luck was about to change. Stopping just inside the door, he scanned the small crowd, and when his piercing gray eyes settled on me, I met them head on. All thoughts of killers and jail time fled from my brain as I let my gaze roam boldly over his body.

Six feet of lean muscle stood there letting me look my fill from his shiny midnight hair to the toes of his well-worn boots. Wide shoulders tapered into a trim waist and flat stomach. Tight jeans encased well-muscled thighs and a promising bulge just below his belt buckle. I returned my gaze to his face and saw full sensuous lips stretched into a wicked grin. Goosebumps actually rose on my skin as I recognized a kindred soul.

Behind the cocky twinkle in his eyes that said he knew I'd enjoyed the visual tour, I saw secrets.

My insides quivered when his gaze pulled away from mine and raked over my curvaceous body. They settled briefly on the length of leg my short skirt showed, before he followed the half dozen guys he was with to a large table with a lazy, almost predatory, gait.

I'd felt that intense gaze on my body as if it were his hands, and loved every second of it. Mary, the waitress who worked the happy hour shift before I came on, had said he was quiet and never responded to her flirting. But he'd certainly responded to mine.

I recognized the group of guys he was with so I loaded up a serving tray with jugs of beer and frosty mugs, then started for their table, intent on learning more about the intriguing stranger.

Maybe the night wouldn't be such a loss after all.

3

"Heads up," I called out, when I reached the table and started passing out mugs. When the last mug was taken from my hand I cocked my hip, and stared directly at him. "Who's the new guy?"

"Lexy, this is Devon," said Dave, a regular, as he clapped a hand on tall, dark, and delicious's shoulder. "I just bought a honey of a bike from him at the Hard Riders Bike Show, and we're going to have some beers to close the deal."

Devon set down his beer and stared right back at me, interest clear in his piercing gaze.

"Welcome, Devon. If there's anything you want here all you need to do is ask, okay?"

He nodded. No smile, no words.

Excitement skittered to my nerve endings, sensitizing my pleasure points in anticipation. The strong, silent type, a true challenge.

"Doesn't mean you'll get it . . . but it never hurts to ask," Jay called out from his spot at the end of the table, reminding me where I was. He winked at me as I walked past him, and I flashed him a fake smile in return.

He'd hit on me a couple of times, but I always turned him down. Jay was a great-looking guy, sexy even. But he gave me the creeps.

Instincts were one of my most important tools, and as much as I wanted to suspect Jay of being the dealer I was looking for, my instincts told me it wasn't him. His creep factor was sexual. The way he looked at me made my skin crawl, and images of weird perverted sex acts flow through my mind. If I were looking for a rapist, or a deviant, he'd be the one I was hunting. But drugs didn't feel right on him.

Instead, I went about serving the few other tables in the pub, ignoring Jay, and letting thoughts of Jimmy's problems get eased out by thoughts of what Devon would look like naked, on his knees between my thighs. I pushed that mental image aside and focused on the fact that he had an edgy quality that told me he was familiar with the darker side of life.

He just might be someone I needed on my side.

"Have a good night." I nodded to the now smiling couple from the back booth as they left for the night. Shifting into waitress mode I gripped a serving tray and went to clear the table. I gathered up the dirty glasses, and the dish that held the unshelled peanuts Jimmy insisted go on every table, and a familiar ripple of excitement shot through my body.

Feeling hot eyes on me, I made sure to bend over far enough when wiping the tabletop for those eyes to get a good look at my firm thighs, and the curve of my ass. I worked hard for my body, and I wasn't above showcasing it if it would get me what I wanted. Straightening up, I glanced over my shoulder and winked playfully at Devon.

When I got back to the bar with a tray full of empties Uncle Tony was waiting for me. Once I'd set the tray on the bar he planted a soft kiss on my cheek. "How's my girl doing?"

"Getting better as the night goes on. And you?"

"I'm worried."

I swallowed a sigh and tried to move around him. Bullheaded Italian macho man that he was, he just shifted and blocked my way. "You can't keep this up, Lexy. It's too dangerous."

This time I didn't bother to hide my exasperation. He looked pretty stubborn standing in front of me, arms crossed in front of his barrel chest, but that didn't matter. I wasn't backing down.

"I'm doing it, Uncle Tony, and nothing you say will stop me." I shook my head and spoke softly, so that only he could hear. "Look, I know you've never understood why I left town, or why I became a P.I. I know you think all I work on are cheating spouses and accident claims, but it's not. Situations like this are exactly why I got into it. I agreed to keep you and Jimmy informed of anything I found out so let me do what I do best."

"You don't know the city anymore." Concern softened his voice as his big rough hands clasped my shoulders and he gave me a little shake. "Things have changed here. The neighborhood isn't the same as when you left. It isn't safe for you to go poking your nose in where it doesn't belong."

White-hot anger flashed through me and I bit my tongue. Self-control was something I'd fought long and hard to learn, and I wasn't going to revert to the uncontrollable, emotional kid of my youth just because I was back in my hometown. Slow deep breaths, and a mental count to ten, saved me from reacting instinctively to his high-handedness.

Uncle Tony was a bachelor who owned and ran a motorcycle repair shop and whose best friend ran a biker bar. He'd been at a bit of a loss as to how to raise a little girl. He never quite understood why I wasn't a typical little girl who liked dolls and dresses, but that didn't mean I wanted to hurt him. He'd done his best by me, and I loved him for it.

"If I don't help him who will? The police?" I kept my voice low, but my scorn was still loud and clear. "As far as they're concerned Jimmy is the man behind a steady flow of junk flowing out of this bar. You think they care if they have the wrong guy? They don't care about justice. They just want to close another case. Jimmy's just another biker to them, and I'm not going to stand by and lose another loved one to their lazy-ass incompetence."

I didn't bother trying to go around Tony again; I pushed past him and stepped behind the bar. "Are you staying for a beer?"

Subject dropped.

Peeking over my shoulder I looked to see if he got the message. He turned to me, shaking his head slowly.

"No, Bella. I already talked to Jimmy, I'm on my way home." He gazed at me, love shining from the depths of his chocolate eyes. "You be careful, okay?"

My shoulders slumped and my anger drained away. "I will."

After watching Uncle Tony leave through the kitchen I turned back to scan the room, and locked eyes with Devon. His face was blank, too blank. I wondered just how much of that little scene he'd observed, and why it mattered.

The kitchen bell rang, signaling that someone's food was up. With a small smile I gave him a flirty finger wave and turned to pick up the munchies. It was time to turn up the heat with him a bit.

Returning to his table with hands full, I deliberately brushed my breasts against the back of his head when I reached past him to set the food on the table. Then walked away without looking back.

A short time later Jimmy came out of his office to see how things were going. He stood in the dark corner just back from the wood of the bar, looking over the room. His smile didn't quite reach his eyes and his thinning hair was mussed, as if he'd been running his fingers through it.

"Need a hand, yet?"

"Sure." I wrapped my arms around thick waist and hugged

him tight. Some people might think it strange that I, a five-foot-three, dirty blonde baby doll look-alike, felt the need to offer comfort to a six-foot-three, two hundred and fifty pound guy covered in tattoos. But both Jimmy and I knew that he loved a good cuddle as much as anybody. Even more so since the shit had hit the fan, because deep down, he didn't have much faith in the cops looking for another suspect either.

Jimmy and Uncle Tony were the only two people from the neighborhood who knew what I did for a living in Vancouver. And even though they *said* they knew I was good at my job, I knew they'd never see me as more than the little girl who had run between the garage and the bar with pigtails, and a wad of bubblegum big enough to choke a horse. I think they even blocked my teenage years from their memories.

"Hey, you two!" A coarse voice shouted from the end of the bar. "Quit cuddling over there and get me a drink, would ya!"

"Shut up, Bear." Jimmy called out above my head, giving me a gentle squeeze before letting me go. "You're just jealous because you know you'll never get your hands on such a fine woman."

Jimmy moved behind the bar and started pouring another draft. The doors to the bar slid open and another couple strolled in. I smiled at them, grabbed my tray and followed them to their table.

Business picked up, and soon I didn't have a chance to think about much of anything except getting the next round of drinks on the table. When I went by Devon's table and noticed that the food was eaten and it was time to clear the plates, my hormones kicked in and my mind went straight back into the gutter.

There was something about being near that man that made any and all thoughts *not* carnal dissolve into thin air. The craving for something wild and erotic surfaced inside me, blending with my need to do *something* to move this case forward.

Leaning forward across the table directly in front of Devon,

I made sure to give him a clear line of vision down my top. Just the sight of him cupping a beer mug in his large hand and the movement of his throat as he swallowed was enough to make my nipples peak. A heavy throb pulsed through me, waking up every pleasure point I had.

I wanted more than his eyes on me.

I wanted those masculine hands with the long fingers stroking my body, and those muscled thighs between mine. And if the heat in his stormy eyes was any indication, I was doing a damn good job of making him want it too. I strolled back to the bar, hips swinging, and juices flowing.

"Jimmy, you see the new guy with Dave and the boys?" I asked as I set a tray of empties on the bar and he started to unload them.

"Yeah. What about him?"

"Do you know him?"

"Seen him around, talked to him a time or two." He concentrated on wiping the glass in his hand and shrugged. "He's pretty quiet, keeps to himself."

Beneath the intense physical attraction I felt for Devon, something about him set off my radar. There was more to him than met the eye.

After that, every time I passed by their table I made a point of rubbing up against Devon in some way. A hand, or a breast, would always make contact. But I still wasn't getting the response I wanted from him. So, the next time I reached to clear an empty beer glass from his table I fumbled it a little, and let it fall right in his lap.

"Oops," I said, batting my eyes and reaching to pick it up. My fingers grazed his denim-covered cock and a sharp hiss slipped through his teeth. "Sorry about that."

"At least it wasn't full," one of the guys called out, obviously thinking Devon's hiss had been surprise, or anger.

"Hey, Lexy," Dave said as he came back from the pool table

and dropped into an empty chair. "You hear the one about Superman being super horny?"

"Nope," I shifted my weight, edging closer to Devon's chair and cocking my hip out as I listened to Dave tell me about how Superman flew around the world asking all the other flying superheroes what to do about his "problem." Seconds later, hot fingers were tickling the back of my knee, trailing lightly up and down the back of my thigh, inching beneath my skirt.

My eyes never left Dave, and my smile never left my face. But the vague words about Superman finding Wonder Woman tanning naked on a beach somewhere barely registered in my brain. Raw need swamped my body just imaging Devon's fingers walking higher and higher up my thigh, to curl into me where I was already wet.

I completely missed the punch line, but joined in the laughter when Dave looked at me expectantly. Pulling myself away from the table, away from those deliciously tormenting fingers, I went up to the bar to fill another order on wobbly legs and try to get my hormones back under control.

And Devon followed.

Standing directly behind me, he leaned around to get the matches he'd asked Jimmy for, and pressed the hard length of his body against mine. Voracious heat surged through me when his breath danced over my ear and his lips brushed my earlobe. "I found something I want."

4

I was so hot and horny after Devon taunted me that even walking, the rubbing of my thighs together, caused tingles to run throughout my aching body.

Enough was enough. Lust was clouding my mind and impatience nipped at my heels. Maybe I could solve two problems with one solution. Find out more about Devon, and slake my lust for him at the same time.

Sauntering up to the men's table I announced that I was going on a short break. "If you need another round before I get back give Jimmy a shout, and he'll bring it over."

With a sultry look and a sharp tug on Devon's nape hairs, I turned and headed to the stock room across from the toilets, and hoped he got the hint.

It was a small room, only about five foot square, full of liquor cases, napkins and mix. Not even room for a chair. I took the ever-present knife from my bra and slid it behind a nearby jar of olives before taking a seat on a case of vodka. With one knee bent I planted my foot on the crate, hiked up my skirt, and scraped a finger across my swollen lips.

I'd give him sixty seconds, and then take the edge off my needs myself.

Thirty seconds later the doorknob turned and Devon slid into the room, closing the door behind him. He just stood and watched for a minute, his hungry eyes glued to the movement of my fingers on my panties. Thoughts of trying to weasel information out of him vanished. I lifted my hand and crooked a finger at him.

He crossed the small space swiftly and reached for me. His calloused fingertips caressed my jaw, his hard body fitting between my thighs as he tugged me roughly to him. Our lips met in a hungry, eating kiss. No subtle seduction here.

My hands ran up his chest and over his shoulders. God! He felt good. So hot and hard, his muscles rippling beneath my touch. Harsh breathing filled the small room as we fought for breath. Devon's tongue invaded my mouth, his hands firm and sure as they swept over my body. He pulled my shirt over my head and my bra down my shoulders, baring me to the waist.

The crate I was sitting on was the wrong height, and I writhed against him unable to get close enough until he lifted me against him, grinding his hardness against my softness. He pivoted and slammed me back against the door. Pinning me there with his body, his lips slid down the curve of my throat to where ripe nipples begged for attention.

His teeth scraped across the hard tips offered up by his own hands. My head snapped back, eyes squeezed tightly shut as I bit my lip to keep from crying out. The sensations were flooding my body from all sides, but I still couldn't get enough.

I wrapped one leg around his hip and ground my core against him, demanding growls bursting from my throat. The rough denim against my inner thigh, and the raised ridge of his zipper rubbing against my panty-clad pussy drove me to the edge, fast.

Grabbing his flanks I pulled him closer, a jolt of annoyance zapping through me. I wanted him closer, deeper, inside me. And I wanted it *NOW*.

Something between a whimper and a frustrated snarl escaped from me and I thrust my hips against him, practically climbing his body. A rough hand slid down the smooth skin of my belly, past the weak barrier of my panties to slip a finger into the slick wetness there. Then it was his turn to groan as he felt how greedily my inner muscles were clutching at him.

"What a hot little bitch you are," he muttered against my skin.

He added another finger and pumped it a few times, the palm of his hand rubbing my clit. A mewling cry flowed from my lips as my orgasm hit. Every muscle tensed and a shock wave of pleasure rippled through my body. When the stars had dissipated from my vision I dragged my hands from his ass to the back of his head and wrapped my fingers around the hair there. Giving it a sharp yank I pulled him away from my well-loved tits, bringing his eyes up to look directly into mine.

"Fuck me," I commanded hoarsely.

"Greedy little thing too, aren't you?" A new light entered his stormy gray eyes and his lips tilted in a half smile.

Something clicked into place and I realized he was right. I didn't want this with him as a way to relieve stress or to forget about any problems. He'd already given me one good orgasm, and there was still an undeniable hunger for more clawing at my insides, and it wasn't for information.

"What can I say?" I said, clenching my inner walls around his fingers. "You feel good."

Looking much too cool and composed for me, he arched an eyebrow and smirked. My thighs clenched tighter around his hips, and I gyrated restlessly against him. "You'll feel even better when you're buried deep inside me."

A deep rumbling laugh echoed in the room as he pulled his hand from between my legs, and set me down on the floor gently. When I was somewhat steady on my feet he stepped back half an inch.

"I have no doubt I will, but when I fuck you it isn't going to be a quick five minutes in the back room."

What the hell? He was saying no?

"Not the first time anyway." His lips brushed against mine, slowly, seductively.

"The first time?"

"Uh-huh. This is just the beginning." A large hand lifted and a calloused fingertip ran gently down my cheek. "What are you doing after work?"

"After work?" I couldn't think. He'd completely thrown me for a loop. My body was humming with an arousal more intense than anything I'd ever felt, and he expected me to think?

With a wicked chuckle he lifted his other hand to his mouth, fingers still glistening with my juices, and sucked them into his mouth. After a heated moment of silence while neither of us moved he drew his fingers out slowly and gave me a little half smile. "You taste good. I'd love to bury my face between your thighs and make you come until you beg me to stop."

Oh!

With a mental head slap I tamped down my inner devil and struggled for control. "You're refusing to fuck me now, and you think I'll give you another chance?"

Another half smile, but this time his eyes lit up. As if my challenge excited him. "You'll give me another chance, tonight too." He stepped back and scooped up my forgotten shirt from the floor, holding on to it while I wiggled my bra back into place.

Snatching the shirt from his hands I tugged it over my head, and brushed back my hair with my fingers. When I felt somewhat restored I struck a pose, shoulders back, chest up, hands planted on my hips. "What makes you so sure of that?"

He stilled, suddenly looking less cocky, and completely serious. "Because we're two of a kind."

With that, he turned on his heel and strode from the room, leaving me shocked and speechless.

5

Stuffing cash into a small, old school-style pencil case, I gave the empty pub a last look-see. Everything was clean and sparkly for the day staff the next morning, and I was more than ready to get out of there.

Heat simmered in my veins at the thought of the night to come. After sticking around for another beer, Devon had left the pub around midnight. He hadn't come back, but I was pretty sure he'd be waiting outside. It would be too cruel for him to throw out a parting comment like he had, and not to be there when I finished work.

Then again, I didn't *really* know him, did I? He could just be that cruel. But I was intrigued enough to not care at this point. He thought we were two of a kind? He thought he knew me well enough to judge something like that? Cocky bastard though he was, I was more than sufficiently enticed.

Striding into the office I tossed the pencil case on Jimmy's desk. It held just over five hundred dollars in cash and various credit slips. Not bad sales for a Monday night, but not good either.

My heart clenched when Jimmy suppressed a sigh and reached for the bag. For a short time there, I'd actually forgotten the real reason I was back in town.

"How bad is it?" I asked.

His mustached lips lifted in a smile but his dark eyes were troubled. "It could be better, baby girl. But it's not all that bad."

"The regulars are still sticking around."

I turned at the sound of a soft voice and saw Wayne leaning against the door to the office.

To look at Wayne you'd never guess he was creeping up on forty. Like most Asians he didn't show his age. The only reason I knew his real age was because I'd first met him on his nineteenth birthday. The same day I showed up on my uncle's doorstep, he'd taken me to Jimmy's for dinner. And even though it had been his birthday, Wayne had insisted on cooking. That was his way.

He'd been working for Jimmy since he dropped out of school when he was fifteen, and he considered Jimmy's kitchen his territory. Therefore, he we was the only one good enough to cook me a "Welcome to the neighborhood" dinner.

The regulars he was referring to were the people who owned the other small businesses in the neighborhood.

It was a small 'hood in the center of town that used to be full of Italian immigrants. In fact, when I first arrived in Edmonton, it was called Little Italy. But now it housed the Asian Market right next to the Italian bakery, and the public phone booths looked like little red pagodas.

Little Italy had gone multicultural.

"The regulars will never give up on you, Jimmy. They know you're innocent." I leaned over the table and gave him a quick, hard hug. "And I won't let the cops railroad you. I promise."

Bending down, I gave Daisy a quick scratch behind the ears and made my way to the front door, determination stiffening my spine.

"You're worried about him, aren't you?" Wayne asked.

"Aren't you? Ever since Mike died, this pub has been all that's kept him going. He can't lose it."

"Is your cab here?"

"No cab tonight, Wayne. A friend is waiting for me."

"Who's this 'friend'?"

Even though Wayne was Chinese, he'd been living and working amongst the macho men so long he couldn't help butting in where it wasn't his business.

"Just a friend that's going to help me relax, and forget my worries for a few hours." I unlocked the door and exited the bar, waiting to hear the click of the lock behind me.

There was a drool-worthy black, red and chrome Indian Spirit parked at the curb in front of the bar. Since I didn't recognize the bike, and there certainly couldn't be many of those beauties around, I guessed it was Devon's. But he wasn't anywhere I could see.

With a glance up and down the street, I took a couple steps and checked around the corner.

The hairs on the back of my neck stood up when I saw a beat-up Ford idling halfway down the alley. Devon was bent over at the waist, passing something inside to the driver. He straightened up, shook his head sharply and patted the roof of the car as he turned to walk back up the street.

I knew the second he saw me. His steps didn't falter, and his posture never changed, but I knew. And I knew it bothered him. The car pulled away quickly, and I cursed the fact that I couldn't read the plate from that distance.

Devon's loose-limbed gait was almost predatory as he came toward me. My heart rate sped up and my nipples hardened at the same time I realized that Devon might just be the man I was looking for, the killer.

My mind raced and my body screamed at me not to think. Thinking was bad. Thinking meant no more mind-blowing orgasms from this man.

Shit!

Our eyes locked as he came toward me and a shiver danced down my spine. A good shiver . . . a yummy shiver of anticipation.

"You all done here?"

I nodded slowly, eyes still locked with his while I tried to get my body back under control and process what I'd just seen. "Who was that?"

He eyed me, his gray eyes sharp and measuring. The look of someone with something to hide. "Just a friend."

"You have a lot of friends that hang out in dark alleys in the middle of the night?"

"Some." His lips tilted up at one corner. "You ready to go?"

We eyed each other for minute, both of us waiting to see what I would do next. Giving myself a mental headshake, I cupped a hand over his groin, and stepped close enough that my lips brushed against his when I answered, "The real question is . . . are *you* ready?"

His hand came up and cupped the back of my head, pulling me that last millimeter until his mouth came down on mine. His fingers clenched and with slow, steady pressure he bent my head back, taking complete control of the kiss.

Firm lips, agile tongue, and sharp teeth ravaged my mouth chasing all thoughts from my mind. My fingers curled inward, gripping him, and I squirmed closer to the hard male body in front of me.

"Ack!"

The sharp cry slipped out when the hand pulled my head back sharply, ripping my mouth away from his, and bringing me back to earth with a slam.

"What do you think, Alexis?" His eyes bore into mine. "Am I ready?"

It was in that moment that I realized I wasn't thinking straight. Hell, I wasn't thinking at all!

My instincts told me Devon was the man I wanted, but not the one I hunted. But for once, I wasn't a hundred percent sure I could trust them.

"I think it's time you take me home."

He planted a hard and fast kiss on my lips before he stepped around me and went for the bike at the curb. He pulled a plain black skullcap out of one of the studded saddlebags and handed it to me before throwing a leg over the bike. Feeling the seductive thrill of danger and lust sweep through me, I climbed on behind him, tucking my skirt under my butt.

It soon became apparent to me that I was stuck between heaven and hell. Being on a motorcycle is always a high. But cradling Devon's hard body between my bare thighs while the low growl of the motorcycle's engine vibrated against my sex was its own kind of purgatory.

As if sensing this, as soon as I directed Devon to the nearby motel where I'd rented a room, he reached for one of my hands and placed it between his legs. Right on the hard cock that I'd been so desperate to ride earlier that night. The whole time my hand explored his size, shape, the fullness of his balls, I wondered exactly who he was, what he'd been up to in the alley, and how the hell he knew my full name was Alexis.

By the time he pulled the bike into the motel parking lot, I had a firm plan in my mind. As much as my body screamed at me, I wasn't inviting Devon in. I might be a bit of a thrill seeker; danger had always turned me on. Sex with a stranger was one thing, but inviting a suspected murderer to my bed wasn't dangerous, it was stupid.

No matter how good he felt I needed to figure out who he was before this went any further. When I'd packed for my return home, I figured my more carnal activities would be curtailed, and packed accordingly. My favorite dildo would have to do.

I pointed, and Devon brought the Spirit to a smooth stop in front of my room door.

He killed the engine and I swung my leg over the bike, coming to stand firm beside him as I undid the safety strap beneath my chin. It was time to do the smart thing and send him on his way. I looked everywhere but at him as I did it too. Foreign nerves, or an overdose of hormones made me clumsy, and my fingers struggled with the simple clasp. Devon swung his own leg over the bike, but remained seated, his booted feet on either side of mine.

"Come 'ere," he said huskily, pulling me to him.

I tilted my head up and let my hands fall to my sides as he made quick work of the helmet. When it slid from my head his fingers gently pinched my chin and pulled my face close to his. After a bruising kiss that took my breath away he gazed deep into my heavy-lidded eyes.

"Last chance to walk away," he said huskily.

6

Of its own accord, my hand clasped his and pulled him to the door behind me.

My fingers trembled when I pushed the key in and twisted the lock. I wasn't sure if it was from arousal or the adrenaline-tinged excitement brought on by the dangerous situation, or a combination of both.

All I knew was that I couldn't seem to say no to this man, or to the carnal hunger he'd awakened inside me.

I stepped into the tiny motel room, flicking the light switch on as I went. The second the door closed behind Devon I turned and pinned him to the wall with my body.

"You are not walking away from me this time." I wrapped my fingers in his hair and pulled his head down until his lips were crushed against mine.

It was as if the three hours since we'd left the storeroom never happened. My body was instantly aflame and I couldn't keep my hands from ripping at his clothes. I shoved his leather jacket off his shoulders and ran my hands over his rippling muscles.

Large hands gripped my ass, lifting me against him so he could carry me to the bed. I landed on my back and bounced once before his body covered mine, making the world disappear in his shadow.

My frantic hands tugged his T-shirt from the waist of his jeans, diving underneath it to get at bare skin.

God, he felt good!

I dragged my mouth away from his, and sucked air deep into my lungs. The sharp nip of his teeth at my neck drove the air right back out in a loud moan.

His weight shifted and my shirt was swept over my head, my skirt and panties pushed down to my ankles where I kicked them away before toeing off my heels. Our hands tangled as I tried to get his belt undone until he finally pushed my hands away.

The bed shifted abruptly, and he climbed off to shuck his own clothing faster than I would've liked. For a second in time, I'd wanted things to slow down enough so I could look my fill. But then he was back, his hot hard body rubbing against my nakedness, his mouth open on mine.

Our tongues dueled, and our hands roamed. Devon settled between my thighs and I felt his cock poking at my mons. I spread wider, hips jerking when firm fingers clamped down on a hard nipple.

"Yes!" A sharp cry ripped from my throat, and I bucked beneath him. The rigid length of his cock slid between my wet folds, rubbing against my extended clit and making me wild. I reached between us and grasped him, rubbing the rounded head firmly through my folds a couple of times before aiming him at my entrance. "Inside me. I want you inside me!"

And then he was in.

My insides stretched around him, molding to his length and thickness as he filled me up. There was a brief second where our gazes locked, and we just enjoyed the ultimate connection. Then he started to move. Slow at first, his cock sliding in and out in a deliciously teasing pace. But I didn't want teasing, I wanted a good hard fuck. I wanted him to be as out of control as I felt. Raking my nails down his back I gripped his tight ass cheeks.

"Faster," I urged him on.

He grunted and buried his head in my neck, picking up speed. I kissed his shoulder, then nipped it sharply while curling my body into his, trying to get the right angle. He was almost there. I canted my hips and bit more and he got the hint. He levered up on his hands and pumped hard and fast, his pubic bone hitting my clit with each thrust, his cock going deep.

"God, woman," he growled, sweat dripping down his cheek. "You're killing me."

Whimpers escaped from my lips as my head thrashed from side to side on the bed. I was so close! My muscles trembled and my orgasm coiled tighter and tighter, low in my belly. But I couldn't reach the peak. An anguished cry emerged from deep inside me as I clawed at Devon's back, writhing beneath him.

The he shifted again, pulling my hands from his back, he slipped his arms under my legs, bending my body so that my knees were against my shoulders, and my hands were pinned to the mattress. My body was curled under his, immobilized as he fucked me furiously.

"Come on, baby. Come for me."

"Yes," I cried out. "That's it. Oh God!"

His cock hit home deep and true with every thrust, his balls banging against my ass. I tugged and tried to get my hands free, I wanted to touch, to claw, to grasp at him, but he wouldn't let go. The odd sense of helplessness pushed me over the edge and the tight knot of excitement in my belly exploded. My pussy clenched and tightened around the shaft inside me, milking it for long seconds as I screamed in pleasure as if for the first time in my life.

"Ahhh." A low guttural groan echoing throughout the room as my own cries faded and Devon's whole body tensed and he let himself go.

It was still dark when I woke up, a heavy arm draped across my waist.

When I realized that I'd fallen asleep immediately, with Devon still next to me, a sharp pain knifed through my chest. I slipped out from under his arm and strode to the bathroom, closing the door behind me.

Struggling for breath, I tried to tamp down the panic rising in my chest, choking off my air. I gave the tap a sharp twist, and splashed cold water on my face.

Breathe . . . breathe.

My heart was pounding in my chest so hard I had to press a chilled hand there to make sure it didn't jump out. I lifted my head and stared at the image in the mirror.

Gone was the cool, confident blonde I was used to seeing, and in her place was a soft-eyed waif who looked lost and alone. The same way I'd looked just before I left town. The stress of the last ten days finally caught up with me, and my face crumpled. Memories long-buried finally surfaced, refusing to be pushed aside any longer.

A younger me, a young man, a happier time. A love so true that when he'd died, I'd wanted to crawl into the grave and be with him forever.

Mike Desmond. Jimmy D's only son. My first lover, my only love, and the only man I'd ever actually *slept* with.

Until tonight.

My knees buckled and I dropped to the floor. Sex was one thing, but actually sleeping curled up to another warm male body was more intimacy than I'd bargained for. Curled up in a tight ball on the cool tiles of the bathroom floor, I cried silently. My mouth opened and closed like a fish gasping for air as tears streamed down my cheeks.

Mike, my heart cried out. I'm sorry. I didn't mean to betray you.

I'd been so careful. Always treating sex as a basic bodily need, an urge. Never letting anyone get too close. But I'd known, deep down, I'd known the moment I saw Devon that he was different.

When he'd strolled into the bar and his gaze had met mine, I'd pretended it was just an animal attraction. Maybe if he'd just fucked me in the storeroom like I'd wanted, I could've walked away.

But he hadn't. And I hadn't been able to walk away from him, even after seeing him in a suspicious light.

My tears slowed, and I breathed deeply. Regaining a modicum of control as my mind woke up. Something inside me trusted him. Trusted him enough to invite him into my room, my body and my bed.

We hadn't used a condom, and I'd fallen asleep next to him.

Those were things that I'd never let happen since loving Mike.

Sitting up, I leaned against the sink cabinet and pulled off some toilet paper. Drawing my knees up to my chest, I blew my nose, and let my head fall back.

I'd learned to always trust my instincts, and now wasn't the time to start doubting them. Not when Jimmy's freedom was at stake. With a heavy sigh I got to my feet and splashed some more cold water on my face. This time I was able to meet my own eyes in the mirror, and only see determination mixed with the sadness there.

I switched the light off before opening the bathroom door and heading back to the bed. I stumbled over something on the floor and cursed quietly. Devon shifted in the bed, but still appeared dead to the world as I stood rooted to the spot, letting my eyes adjust to the darkness before going any farther.

When I could see better I eyed the bundle of clothes I'd almost tripped over, and then glanced back at the still form on the bed. Before I could think too hard, I scooped up the bundle and strode back to the bathroom.

I flicked the light on and the door shut behind me again before quickly and silently searching the pockets of Devon's jeans. Keys and a couple of condoms in one pocket. His wallet in another. Seems he'd at least *planned* to be safe. Feeling no shame whatsoever I rifled through the wallet. Driver's license, cash, a picture of a dog. That was it. No credit cards, no bank cards, no membership cards for movie rentals or grocery stores.

I put everything back in his pockets, turned the light out and left the bathroom again, dropping his jeans on the floor by the bed before crawling back onto the mattress.

For a long time I just lay there, mulling over things. The lack of the usual collection of plastic in Devon's wallet seemed odd.

My eyes drifted closed, my subconscious still working on the puzzle. The body next to me shifted closer, the heavy arm drifting around my waist again and pulling me close. I gave in to the warmth growing in my belly and snuggled into the shelter provided, feeling safe for the first time in a long time.

A kiss on the neck and my name whispered in my ear by a husky male voice woke me up the next morning with the knowledge of who, and what, Devon was, fresh in my mind.

7

I fought to remain pliant, kept my eyes closed, and tried to figure out what to do. One result of never sleeping with a man after sex is I've never had to deal with the morning after before. Add to that the fact that both Devon and I had some serious secrets, so I had no clue what to do.

Devon nuzzled in by my ear, his hot breath sending a pleasurable shiver rippling through me. Both of us lay on our sides, with Devon spooned behind me. I could feel his erection poking against my lower back, as one of his hands palmed a breast. He pulled and pinched at the nipple, bringing it awake with the promise of attention.

I struggled to think of something to say as he worked my body. Licking, nibbling and sucking at my neck, his hand shifted from one breast to the other, his hips rocking gently against mine. Within seconds any thoughts of identities and occupations that were rattling around my head fled.

He shifted closer as I dropped an open hand behind me and caressed his hip. Reaching past that, I gripped his downy cheek and pulled him closer. Sharp teeth nipped playfully at the tendons between my neck and shoulder, his hand leaving my breast to graze over my belly and between my legs. The light brush of his fingers wasn't enough. Bending my knee, I lifted my leg and gave him full access to my heated sex.

A growl of approval sounded near my ear and my fingers tightened, digging my nails into his ass in reaction and pushing back against him some more. My silent urging did the trick and Devon shifted again. His foot slipped between my legs and I felt him poking at my entrance. His teasing fingers deserted me to guide himself, and soon he was slowly sliding inside, filling me up and dragging a soft moan from my throat.

We rocked together in a slow, steady rhythm, Devon's hand skimming up my side. He clasped my wrist and lifted my arm away from him, over my head. When it was alongside the one I'd rested my head on in sleep he wrapped his other hand around both of mine, pinning them lightly, leaving my body completely open for his other hand to explore.

Fire followed wherever that hand went as he cupped my breasts, pinched my nipples, and skimmed over my belly to tickle my clit. The bedsprings squeaked as Devon's pace picked up a bit of speed, blending with the little sighs and moans that crawled out from between my lips. Tension coiled in my core and Devon's fingers tightened around my wrist when I tried to pull a hand away. Not having any control, just lying there getting fucked leisurely, unable to touch or play, was incredibly erotic.

And more intimate than I wanted.

I leaned my upper body forward, and thrust my hips back. "Faster," I muttered. "Deeper."

A calloused hand cupped the inside of my knee and lifted, opening me up as he followed through.

I pressed my face against the mattress and moaned loudly. He hit the sweet spot deep inside me every time. My cunt clenched around him, sucking at him hungrily every time he pulled out. My eyes shot open and my body tensed as pleasure erupted from deep inside and spread hotly throughout my body. Devon dropped my leg, dropped my hip and thrust deep, holding me tight against him as his cock jerked and twitched inside me, his grunt mingling with my muffled whimpers.

The room slowly came into focus and I realized that Devon was still pressed up against me, and his cock was still inside me, keeping us connected. With slow, deliberate movements I pulled away, and headed for the bathroom.

A couple minutes later I emerged with hair combed, face and teeth washed, and mental armor in place. Devon had pulled on his pants and was standing shirtless by the window, peeking around the curtain. He turned when I entered the room and watched me walk naked to the dresser. I pulled out a pair of sweatpants and a tank top. I dressed quickly and efficiently, then leaned against the dresser and returned his steady gaze.

"Good morning," he said softly.

"Morning," I answered. I gave him a small smile. "We need to talk."

He bent down and picked up his T-shirt. "About?"

I suppressed my disappointment as he pulled his shirt on and I lost sight of his washboard abs. There'd been a forced casualness in his one word answer. One that most people probably wouldn't pick up on, but my internal radar told me he was girding his inner defenses the same way I'd done in the bathroom minutes earlier.

In that instant I decided that head-on was the wrong tact to take with him. Questioning him about his late-night back-alley activities and demanding answers about who he was wasn't the way to go. Instead I tackled another subject. "We didn't use a condom."

"Yeah, we got a bit carried away there." He blew out a sharp breath and eyed me as he zipped his jeans and buckled his belt. "I can assure you I was given a clean bill of health only a couple weeks ago, and unprotected sex isn't the norm for me."

I believed him.

"Me either." I looked away. "Not since I was seventeen anyway. And I am on the pill, so birth control is covered."

When he had his boots and jacket on he strolled over to me and stroked a finger down my cheek. "I'd like to see you again."

My pussy throbbed at his words, and my heart kicked in my chest at the look in his eyes. I ignored both and focused on why I was in Edmonton at all.

"I'd like that." I wrapped my arms around his waist and smiled at him. "Do you have to work today? What is it you do anyway?"

He bent forward and gave me a small kiss. "I'm a private dealer. I buy and sell collectables to private parties, anything with an engine. And yes, I have to work for a bit today, but I'll drop by the bar and we can make plans. Okay?"

I stepped on my tiptoes and pressed myself against him, lifting my mouth to his for another kiss.

Strong arms wrapped around me and gentle lips fused with mine. His tongue dipped inside my mouth for a quick tease and then he was gone, striding to the door.

He stopped in the open door and turned. "I'll take that as a yes." With a wink and wicked smile he was gone.

"I don't like it."

"You don't need to like it. You don't even need to do anything, Tony! In fact, that's exactly what I want. I want you to *not* do anything."

Frustration made my voice louder, and harsher, than I'd meant it to be.

"Hey guys, calm down." Jimmy was quick to remind us where we were. He looked from Tony, who stood next to him, to me, standing feet braced wide and hands on hips, in front of his desk. "Tony's just worried about you, baby girl. He overheard a couple of bikers talking about you over at the shop this morning, and it's caused some concerns. For both of us."

"Bullshit." I wasn't going to let them do the "I'm a man I know best thing." "You two have had 'concerns' about me doing this from the start. Don't use the fact that some guys were talking trash about me as an excuse to try and tell me what to do."

"It was more than just trash talk, Alexis." Uncle Tony was getting stressed. I could see his Italian temper throbbing in the small vein at his temple. Strangely, knowing he was getting upset had a calming effect on me. "They knew too much about you. They know you started work here the day you arrived in town—"

"Everyone knows that." I waved it away.

"They know you're searching for a drug hook-up—"

"Everyone knows that too. How else am I going to find who's dealing at our back door?"

He threw his hand up in the air. "They know what motel you're staying at."

"I haven't kept that a secret." A chill rippled down my spine. I hadn't told anyone where I was staying.

"They knew you had a guest who stayed all night last night." This time his voice got quiet, deadly. I knew his anger was toward the guys yapping about me, but the parental disapproval radiating from him was directed at me.

It was strange. I hated the heavy-handed father routine, but it warmed my insides to know he still cared enough to disapprove.

"You've known I'm not a virgin since you caught me and Mike when we were fifteen." God, what an embarrassing scene that had been! Growing up running between my uncle's bike shop and his best friend's bar, I knew more about what men thought of sex by the time I was thirteen than most women know when they're thirty. The guys had never been shy around me. However, my uncle had somehow managed to convince himself I was a princess until the day he'd caught me naked with Mike. If Jimmy hadn't been there I think Tony would've killed Mike, even though they were like family. The shock of seeing us naked in bed had lit a fire under his temper.

Tony got over it, but he'd always think of me as his princess.

"This isn't about the fact that you had sex, Lexy! It's about the fact that you had it with a guy who's aroused just as much interest as you have." Jimmy spoke up from behind his desk. "A man that showed up here around the same time you did."

That didn't surprise me. Well, in truth, it didn't surprise me that he showed up two days after the stabbing in the back alley, the fact that he was there at all *did* surprise me. Especially if he was who I thought he was.

"Speaking of Devon, what do you know about him, Tony?"

He glanced at Jimmy before answering me. "Nothing much. Why?"

"I asked Jimmy last night, but he didn't know much either. Has he been in the shop? He says he's a dealer for a small group of private collectors. Bikes, cars, anything with an engine. If he really is, then I'd think at least one of you would've met him before. That he'd have come in to either the bar, or the detailing shop at some point to see who's got what in the area."

"He came in once, a little over a week ago. But with the bike show yesterday, it's not surprising he hasn't been in since."

"I hate to say this, but I think it's time we talk to the cops." Jimmy shook his head at his own words and shrugged at the way my eyebrows jumped.

"And tell them what exactly? That there's no way they

could believe you'd stab a drug addict and leave him to die in the alley because your son was one?" My insides trembled, and my blood started to boil. "They know that! They know that Mike died of an overdose. And they didn't care! They didn't even bother to look for the dealer who sold him those bad pills."

Uncle Tony reached for me, but I shrugged his hands off my shoulders. I was quickly losing my grip and it would be too easy to let those strong arms comfort me. And then they'd never trust me to figure any of this out.

"Just because the cops screwed up your parents' case doesn't mean they'll screw this one up. I don't like it any more than you do, but we need help, and you have to learn to trust someone, sometime, Lexy." Tony's voice was quiet and firm, making it clear to me that the two men had already discussed this option between themselves.

Disappointment at their lack of faith in me made my heart ache. But I wasn't giving up.

"I'm not taking a chance that the real killer will go free, and Jimmy will go to jail. When Mom and Dad's killers walked, I was a kid. There was nothing I could do about it." I met Tony's gaze head on. "Then."

"What does that mean?"

I bit my tongue. Tony had loved his brother and sister-in-law, but he also had a healthy respect for the police, and the law. He'd never understand the justice I'd sought as an adult. "Nothing. It just means that this time around there's something I can do about things."

"What are you going to do that the cops can't do? Why are you so against trusting them?"

"Why are you so bent *on* trusting them? I know you wanted to be a cop, Tony, but how can you possibly trust an organization that thinks that if you've got flat feet you can't enforce the law?" Resignation washed over me and I swallowed a sigh. Might as well tell them, maybe they'd back off a bit. "Besides, I think it's too late."

"Huh?"

I flopped into the chair in front of Jimmy's desk. The one I'd ignored because sitting in it would've made me feel subservient to them when we'd been arguing. Now it just made me feel like a kid getting chewed out by the school principal. "I think Devon's a cop."

"What makes you say that?" Jimmy spoke first. Tony and he looked at each other, then at me. "In fact, how can you be sure he's not the killer? He did tell you he was a bike dealer."

Pursing my lips I shook my head resolutely. "No, he's not the killer. That much I'm sure of."

"How can you be so sure?"

Would these two men ever see me as more than their little girl? Even after ten years away from home they couldn't seem to accept that I was an adult, let alone a professional P.I. and skip tracer with a great track record. Aggravation bubbled up again, but I bit my tongue.

"I just am. Do you really think I'd let a murder suspect in my bed?" I ignored the fact that I hadn't been a hundred percent sure of Devon's innocence before I'd slept with him and searched his wallet. They didn't need to know that. "Ask me why I think he's a cop."

"Why do you think he's a cop?"

There was a funny note in Tony's voice when he asked me, but I couldn't put my finger on what was off.

"He's working at getting in with the regulars here, he carries no I.D. in his wallet other than a driver's license, and I saw him talking to someone in a beat-up Ford in the back alley after we closed last night." I looked at them expectantly. "And he wasn't pleased that I saw him."

"Shit!" Jimmy clapped his hand on top of his head and let out a big sigh.

"Don't worry, Jimmy. I told you, I've got it under control. I'm going to find out what he knows."

"How are you going to do that?"

I just arched an eyebrow at him and tried not to smirk. "I have my ways. Don't worry about it."

8

The sun was bright and the streets were full when I left The Crib with a confident bounce in my step that was completely fake. Emotions roiled about inside me, and I struggled to sort them into compartments in my mind. I knew I needed to deal with everything that had been going on; I'd been in denial for too long and it was all catching up to me.

Tony and Jimmy were worried I would get myself into a situation where I might get hurt. They didn't realize that I was already there. Just being back in Edmonton, back in the neighborhood, had put me in that place.

Physical danger didn't scare me. Hell, I loved the rush of pitting myself against the unknown, and the fact that my survival instincts were honed enough that I usually came out on top. I'd been hurt, and I have the scars to prove it. But the physical scars were nothing compared to the emotional ones burned into my soul.

My gaze traveled over the various storefronts as I strode south, toward the river. I needed to get away from the old neighborhood. The one that wasn't anything like I remembered it, yet, still held the power to remind me of a time when I thought things could be normal, that *I* could be normal.

I reached Jasper Avenue and kept on going. The North Saskatchewan River cut right through the middle of the city and was surrounded by parkland full of bike trails and picnic spots. The River Valley was my destination. I managed to keep my mind blank by concentrating on my footsteps. Falling back into the comfort of counting them to distract me from my thoughts. Until I reached a small grove of trees just off the beaten path.

It was the spot where Mike kissed me for the first time, and made me feel something other than anger for the first time in years. I was thirteen, he was fourteen, and he'd followed me there after I'd had a fight with Tony about something stupid. Tony and I had fought often. When I arrived at his house, a newly orphaned, surly ten-year-old, he hadn't known what to do with me. He wanted me to be what he thought a typical little girl should be, and I just wanted to be left alone.

Guilt over not being at home when my parents were killed had eaten me up as a kid. It wasn't until years later, on that fateful day when Mike had kissed me, that he finally made me see my parents would be happy I was at a friend's sleepover when our house had been broken into. That as much as I would've liked to have died with them, they wouldn't have wanted it.

It was as if Mike's spirit were still in that spot. I wandered over to it and wiped the silent tears from my cheeks as I dropped to the ground. Leaning back against the tree I raised my eyes to the cloudless sky.

"Why, Mikey? Why did you want to even try them?" A heavy sigh eased its way past my tight throat. He knew how I felt about drugs. He knew I blamed my parents' murders on the fact that the guys who had broken into their house were doing it to steal so they could get their next fix. Their drug use had made them not care about the lives they took.

I guess that was why he'd felt the need to try the drugs on his own, and not tell me what he was doing.

To know that popping a few pills could take away the light and laughter of him in my life was even more reason to hate drugs. I knew Jimmy felt the same way. He'd never been one to let that sort of thing into his bar, but when Mike had over-dosed, he'd become a vocal antidrug supporter. The city police knew this too. It was why I just couldn't understand why they'd suspect him of stabbing a known addict in the back alley. If it had been a dealer, then Jimmy would be a reasonable sus-pect, but not an addict. He was too well known for trying to save addicts.

It just didn't make sense. When I really thought about it, an undercover cop's presence, Devon's presence, in the bar didn't make sense. There had to more to it.

A couple of hours later I arrived at the bar for my shift. It was so slow that Jimmy sent Mary, the other waitress, home right away. She wasn't pleased, but there wasn't anything she could do about it either. Business being so slow didn't sap my determination; in fact it did just the opposite. When Smelly Tim came in and pulled up a stool at the bar, I filled a frosted pint with draft and headed over to him.

"Hey, Tim. How're you doing?"

"Beat. I've had a shit day at work, Lexy. This beer is going to hit the spot." He took a long pull from the mug before putting it down and giving me the opening I'd been waiting for. "And you, how're you doing?"

"Well . . ." I leaned on the bar, and gave him a private smile. "To be honest, I could use a pick-me-up."

He sipped his beer, watching me with small sharp eyes, and I breathed through my mouth so I wouldn't gag at the smell of being so close to him. When he didn't respond I stepped back and took a casual stance.

"So what is it you do anyway? For work, I mean?"

"I work at the hospital."

"Really?" Easy access to drugs there. "Doing what?"

"I work in the kitchen. It's hot as hell in there at times. I swear, sometimes I think I'm in hell instead of Edmonton General."

"All kitchens are like that. No matter where you work."

With a glance at the end of the bar I spotted Wayne leaning against the wood watching one of the big-screen televisions. Poker. What was with the new poker phenomena? I didn't get it.

The two men fell into an easy discussion about the temperature of the ovens and how the ovens ranked up the heat in the kitchens. I wandered away and thought about what I'd learned, and what I already knew.

Smelly Tim's job at the hospital, even if in the kitchen, could certainly give him the connections to get drugs. He couldn't make much as a cook, so the money to be made from dealing had to be a huge temptation. I went through the bar; rag in hand, dusting things, trying to keep busy. However, I checked him out from every angle. The guy had a knife tucked into his boot, only visible if you were looking for it, and he carried a small backpack. Not unusual among bikers, but still, I really wanted to get a look at what was in that bag.

With a sigh, I threw my shoulders back, fluffed my hair and got ready to use my best assets to get what I wanted.

"Hey, Tim." I sidled up to the bar, close to him, and laid my hand on his sleeve. "Did you ever find a party for me?"

He turned his head from the TV and didn't bother to hide the fact that he couldn't take his eyes off my cleavage. The gleam in his beady eyes had me repressing a shiver.

"Not yet," he drawled. He glanced around the bar for the first time. "Where's Mary? I thought she was working tonight."

A light bulb flickered to life inside me. Was she his connection here? Is that how The Crib was involved?

He interrupted my thoughts, leaning closer and whispering in my ear, "I think I can line something up for tonight if you're interested."

Forcing a naughty grin to my lips I stepped back a bit, and nodded eagerly. "That would be great."

The door swung open and a couple of guys headed straight for the pool tables. I grabbed some coasters and followed to get their drink order. When I got back to the bar Tim pushed aside his empty pint glass and waved at me.

"I'm out of here. I'll call you about that party."

As soon as he was out the door I shook off the twinge of unease creeping up my neck.

"You think it's him?"

I turned to Jimmy, who'd come up behind me. He could move pretty quietly for a big guy. "He's sleazy enough. He works at the hospital, which gives him access to drugs. He's friends with Mary, I think, and he comes in here often enough to get a handle on things. What do you think?"

"I think you better call me before you meet him for any party. I get that you don't want to work with the cops, but you are not doing this alone, you hear me?"

With a gentle pat on his shoulder and a small smile, I assured him I'd call him if I heard from Tim. I knew I was lying, and I was pretty sure Jimmy knew too, but he let the matter drop.

Devon came in for dinner around eight. I was at another table when he strolled in, but I couldn't help but enjoy the view as he passed me on his way to the back of the room. He had a great ass, covered in faded denim and framed perfectly with well-worn leather chaps, it was a shame to lose the view when he sat down in a booth by himself.

When I was done giving change to my customers I headed to his table. My muscles tensed a bit more with each step and I played greetings through my mind. Part of me wanted to call him out as a cop, but if I did that, I might lose any chance of helping Jimmy out. For the first time in my life, I wasn't able to meet things head-on. I didn't know how to deal with him.

But there was no hiding now.

"Hey there, sexy," I said, flashing a bold smile. No way was I going to let him have a clue how unsettled I was. "How was your day?"

"Could've been worse." His gaze swept over my face, lingered on my lips for a second. When his eyes returned to mine I could see the embers of lust flickering to life in the gray depths. "But it's getting better."

Arousal licked at my insides and my smile turned genuine. I was on familiar ground now.

Cocking a hip out and bracing it against the table I trailed a fingertip playfully across my collarbone to the top button on my blouse. "I can make it downright . . . satisfying, if you give me a chance."

The embers turned to flames and my body heated in an all-over flush as we just looked at each other. Tension and stress flowed from my body and my heart rate jumped a gear. It was as if he could see inside me. See all my secrets and all my flaws, and they didn't change a thing. He still liked what he saw. He still wanted me.

"I'll pick you up when the bar closes, and you can give it your best try." Full lips tilted into a wicked grin. "But for now, a beer and a burger will do."

When Devon's food was ready I brought it to him, and sat for a bit. There were still only a couple of tables occupied in the bar, and no word from Smelly Tim on a party, so I had the time.

It was strangely comfortable. We talked about movies.

Music and books. We had a lot more in common than I ever would've expected. It was only when he commented on not being a native Albertan that I saw an opening to find out more.

"What brought you to Edmonton then?"

"Work." He munched a french fry before continuing. "A friend of mine was in the same business and he called me up when he got busy enough to need a partner."

"Did you leave anyone behind? Friends, family, loved ones?" The words were casual but the nudge in my belly told the real story. I wanted to know just how alike we were.

I didn't have friends, or lovers, in Vancouver. Just a few coworkers I'd share a drink with every now and then. It was all good though because I preferred my life that way. Part of me had always been aware that after Mike's death I'd shut my emotions off. It was easy to psychoanalyze myself and see that I didn't want to let anyone get too close. Every time I dropped my guard, someone I cared about got hurt. So it was best for everyone if I just didn't care.

"Nope." His shoulders lifted and fell in a casual shrug. "My parents are happily retired and traveling in a motor home somewhere and my business partner is the only friend I care to keep in touch with."

I nodded. It sounded like we were of the same mind. Emotional ties were something to be avoided.

Hell, it's why I never made my way back to Edmonton after tracking down the thieves who killed my parents. Part of me figured I was as bad as they, and didn't deserve to be loved and cared about. But the bigger part just didn't care. I hadn't killed them. I'd just dangled the bait, and they'd been stupid enough to go for it.

The fact that the bait was a business owned by a local Hell's Angels chapter was something they should've considered. Everyone knew you didn't steal from them and get away with it.

Now their bodies would never be found, and my conscience tickled me at times, but my soul felt a bit of peace at knowing my parents' killers had finally paid for what they did.

I watched Devon from under my lashes as he pushed away his plate and reached for his wallet. He could be real trouble for me. He'd said we were two of a kind, and he might be right. Neither of us wanted emotional entanglements, yet, we didn't seem to be fighting this intense pull between us either.

What exactly was going on here? Would he understand why I did what I did? Did I care?

He was a cop, but there was a basic animal quality about him that told me he probably bent the rules himself a time or two. That could be a good thing in the end. Then again, a good thing might be me finding a better way to keep tabs on him other than letting him into my bed again.

"Well?" he asked quietly.

"Well, what?"

"You looked pretty deep in thought there for a few minutes. I figured you were trying to think of a way to back out of seeing me again."

My spine stiffened and I let out a slow chuckle. I might've been thinking that, but there was no way I'd let him know it. "Baby," I stood up and reached for the empty plate, "I'm going to do so much more than *see* you again."

The heat of his gaze flowed over my curves as I walked away from the table, swinging my hips and listening to his own low laugh.

Oh yeah, he was trouble.

9

"Strip."

We'd just entered my motel room and I'd gone straight to the bedside table to flick on the lamp, but froze at his command. My heart kicked in my chest and my nipples hardened to the point of pain.

I turned on my heel and watched Devon shrug out of his leather jacket before he dropped into the upright chair just inside the door. If any other man had spoken to me in that tone, I'd kick his ass. But the flicker of tenderness lurking below the heat in Devon's intense gaze made his attitude exciting, not demeaning.

Reaching up, I played with the top button on my blouse. Keeping my eyes on him I moved from one to the next, slipping them through the holes, without moving closer to him or saying a word. When my blouse hung open I slipped one hand under the cloth and cupped a breast. Scraping my fingertip across the nipple it stiffened even more, aching for a firmer touch.

"Take it off. The bra too." Devon's voice was husky with

arousal, his own hand drifting over his groin to make an adjustment. "I want to see you touch yourself."

With slow, sure movements I slipped the blouse from my
shoulders, and removed the black push-up bra I'd been wearing. Biting my lip, I closed my eyes and held the weight of a
breast in each hand, squeezing lightly while I pinched my nipples between finger and thumb.

Arrows of pleasure shot from nipple to groin and a sigh of
longing spilled from my lips. It felt good, but I wanted him.

I cracked my eyes open and watched him watch me as I
reached back and undid the clasp on my skirt. With a little
shimmy of my hips the skirt dropped to the ground and I stood
in front on him naked, but for my thong and my shoes.

Unwilling to let him know just how much I wanted him to
touch me, I sat on the edge of the bed across from him and
spread my legs crudely.

I sucked a finger into my mouth for a brief second before
trailing it down the center of my chest, across my belly and beneath the elastic edge of my panties. Devon's lips parted and his
tongue darted out as he watched the movement beneath the
black lace.

"How does it feel?" he asked.

"So good," I whispered, shocking myself by answering him,
egging him on. "Slick and wet. Ready to be filled."

A low groan rumbled out of him and he made quick work of
the buckle of his chaps, as well as his jeans. In seconds he had
both pushed low on his hips and his cock bobbed out in the
open, hard, thick and proud. Saliva pooled in my mouth as his
fingers stroked it lightly up and down.

"Take off your panties."

I hesitated for a second, and his eyes met mine. "Please."

Some men might think saying please to a woman made them
less, but Devon was confident and assured, and the word flow-

ing from his lips only made me want to do whatever he asked. With one quick move I was rid of the thin lace.

"Get back on the bed," he instructed. "Sit against the wall, spread your legs. I want to be able to see everything."

Excitement skittered through me as I did what he asked. My brain had shut off and I was reduced to a mass of quivering desire, seeking only pleasure and praise.

I propped a pillow up against the headboard and leaned back. Drawing my knees up I kept them spread wide. Devon's cheeks flushed and the hunger on his face was clear to see. I felt crude and dirty, and desired and *wanted*.

"Show me how you please yourself," he rasped. "Make yourself come for me."

One hand immediately dipped between my legs, straight for the hard bud of flesh that peeped out from its protective hood. My other hand cupped a breast and played with the nipple. Tension coiled low in my belly and my hips tilted forward a bit, seeking firmer pressure.

Devon's hand circled his rigid shaft completely and he stroked himself, the head of his penis turning a deeper purple and starting to shine deliciously. A low moan eased from my throat and I rubbed my button harder, the knot in my belly tightening fiercely.

"That's it, baby. I can see your pussy working."

Keeping the steady pressure on my clit with one hand, my other traveled across my belly to join it between my legs. I let my knees fall outward and I was completely open as my hips thrust up to welcome a stiff finger inside me.

"Oh," another helpless moan escaped from me. "I'm close. So close, Devon."

"I know, babe. I can see how wet you are. I can smell you from here. You smell so good."

Those earthy words, uttered in his deep husky voice, pushed

me over the edge. I dug my heels into the bed and thrust my hips forward. One finger thrusting inside while the other frigged my clit. My eyes slid shut on the vision of his fist pumping faster as the knot in my belly expanded and a long, low cry eased from my lips.

When my heart rate slowed and the pounding in my ears subsided I opened my eyes to see Devon still seated in the chair. He wasn't stroking himself anymore. Instead, his hands were resting on leather-clad thighs, and his eyes were burning with a raw male hunger that set my blood to near boiling again.

"Come here."

My recent orgasm was forgotten and my body clamored for more attention. The brief remembrance that I didn't take orders from men was pushed away, and I scrambled off the bed. Without waiting for any more words from him I dropped to my knees between his legs and eagerly took him in my mouth.

A hiss of pleasure echoed through the room and Devon rested a hand on the back of my head. Gripping the base of his shaft with one hand, I took as much of him in as I could. He hit the back of my throat before I slowly pulled back with steady suction. When I got to the top I swirled my tongue around the swollen head and tasted his unique flavor.

"Oh yes," he whispered, stroking my hair back and shifting his hips under me. "That's it, baby."

After that initial taste a tinge of awkwardness overcame me. He felt big and full and foreign in my mouth. But the urge to please him was stronger than any inhibitions I had so my eyes closed and I stroked him up and down with my mouth. The throbbing ridge on the underside fascinated me, and my tongue rode it while my hand sank lower to fondle his furred balls.

A loving male hand rested under my chin while the other flexed in my hair. I could feel his tension mounting, his cock growing harder and thicker as I continued to love him. Trying

desperately to breathe as I picked up the pace, I inhaled his
musky scent. His hips lifted toward me and a whimper escaped
my throat.

Suddenly, the hand wrapped in my hair urged me upward.
Releasing him from my mouth with a loud pop, I crawled up
his body and met his open-mouth kiss with mindless passion.
Spreading my legs, I straddled him on the chair and impaled
myself on his hardness.

Mingled sighs and groans filled the air as I pulled my mouth
from his and rolled my hips. The leather of his chaps cool and
smooth against the backs of my thighs, making our connection
that much hotter. Hands gripping his shoulders I rested my
forehead against his. Our bodies moved in perfect rhythm together, our gazes locked. I concentrated on the feel of him sliding in and out.

The chair was low enough that my feet were planted firmly
on the floor. I shifted the angle slightly and my pussy spasmed
at the new depth of penetration.

"You feel so damn good," he muttered. Large hands gripped
my hips and his thighs tensed beneath me.

Another slight shift and he was settled deep inside me, and
all I had to do was roll my hips. He filled me, stretching me to
fit him perfectly as my insides clenched and tightened with
every move. My clit rubbed against his pubic bone and everything I had was concentrated on the tight knot of pleasure that
was trying desperately to burst free. A desperate whimper
burst from my lips and I tossed my head back.

"Come on, Lexy," Devon growled, leaning forward and
nipping at my neck. "I can feel you. You're almost there. God
you're so tight."

His lips nibbled down my chest, and sucked a hard nipple
into his mouth. Worrying it between his teeth, he sent pleasure
bolts darting through me.

"Ahhh," I gasped. "Please . . . Devon! Please . . . I can't . . . arghhh!"

I knew I wasn't making any sense but I didn't care. My hips were pumping furiously and my fingers were digging into his muscles. I leaned forward to try another angle and heard him gasp at the shift. One hand left my hip and he cupped a breast, pinching and pulling at the nipple ruthlessly while his mouth was back on my neck. His hot breath skimmed over my ear as he panted.

"Fuck, you're hot!"

A mewl of mixed passion and frustration escaped from me. I couldn't even form proper words. But it was as if he could read my body better than I could. His mouth became ravenous on my neck, licking and biting, but not hurting. His other hand slid into the crease of my ass. A fingertip pressed gently at my rear entrance, sliding in and pushing me over the edge into oblivion as a sharp scream of pleasure ripped from my throat.

When the world righted itself again Devon was getting up from the chair. "Shhhhh," he crooned when I stirred and attempted to climb off him. "I've got you."

He stood, one arm across my hips, the other across my back, his hand cradling my head against his shoulder. With a couple of steps he was at the edge of the bed. He tugged the blankets down and stretched me out on the cool sheets. I lay there, a boneless pile of satisfied female as I watched him rid himself of his clothes.

He was so beautiful, masculine and dangerous-looking in his denim and leathers. His hair was mussed from my fingers and dark stubble shadowed his jaw, but his gray eyes glowed with warmth and tenderness as he climbed into bed and pulled me close.

"We need to talk soon," he whispered before I drifted off on a cloud.

* * *

The shrill beeping of my cell phone jerked me awake a short time later. In an automatic move I snatched the phone from the bedside table and flipped it open.

"Hello?" My voice was a bit hoarse from my screams of pleasure earlier, but with a glance at the clock I knew most people would assume it was husky from sleep.

"Lexy?" A male voice questioned. "You still want to party?"

My mind jerked awake. "Tim?"

"Yeah, I got a friend here that's willing to party with us if you're still interested."

I glanced at the neon digits on the alarm clock. Almost three A.M. "Now?"

"It too late for you? I figured you'd just be getting off work."

It was a reasonable assumption. But the bar had been so quiet, with no customers other than Devon from eleven o'clock on, that just after midnight Jimmy had told me to go home early. I slipped from the bed and peeked at Devon, who lay unmoving in the middle of the bed. "No, no, it's not too late. I'm just surprised. Where's the party?"

There was no way I was going to let an opportunity to get at the dealer pass me by. I went into the bathroom and closed the door while he gave me an address. Definitely not the safest part of town, I thought when I hung up. Creeping into the room again I took a pair of stretch jeans from the closet and pulled them on without underwear. Devon sighed and rolled over when I took a lycra undershirt from a drawer and put it on.

Reaching for my own leather jacket I hesitated, eyeing his sleeping form. The urge to wake him up and tell him what I was doing was strong. So strong my fingers started to tremble and I had to count to ten before I could pull on socks and lace up my boots.

I was used to working alone and depending only on myself. Devon did seem to know me, and my body, better than anybody. But that didn't mean I could trust him to watch my back. Reaching into the corner of the drawer I drew out a beautiful butterfly knife and slid it into the waistband of my jeans. Running my fingers through my hair, I stuffed my phone in my jacket pocket and went for the door, prepared for the worst and hoping for the best.

10

The cab pulled up to the curb and I slid out of the car. The house was a small clapboard one, old, but not dilapidated. There were lights blazing, a couple of cars in the driveway, but no people lingering outside, or any outward signs of a party. Heading up the walkway I scanned the yard, noting that there was no fence around the house, just a privacy hedge separating it from the house next door. Muffled strains of music could be heard, and a couple of voices, but I still saw no shadows or movement in the house.

The hairs at the back of my neck prickled, and I checked to make sure my knife was in place before straightening my spine, and knocking on the door. It swung open almost immediately, and Tim leered at me from inside.

"Come on in, doll." He stepped back and waved me into the room. "We've been waiting for you."

He must've showered after work because for once I couldn't smell the usual rancid body odor when I stepped past him. A quick scan of the room showed me two other guys, a coffee table full of tobacco and weed, and a clean view of the back door. The house itself wasn't too bad, messy and the furniture was old and well worn, but it also had an almost . . . family feel to it.

Moving into the room I positioned myself on the arm of a sofa, making sure I still had a clear path to each of the exits. Comfortable as the house was, the hairs on the back of my neck were still twitching, and I was still working.

"Hey," I nodded to the others.

Tim shut the door and came to sit on the sofa next to me. With too much familiarity he placed a grimy hand on my thigh and grinned up at me. "You ready to party?"

The size of his pupils told me he'd started the party without me. He wasn't too whacked out, but he was high enough that he'd probably believe whatever I said.

"You bet," I replied. "I've been ready for a while now."

"You prefer a joint or the bong?" He waved at the table and its contents. There was a pipe, a plastic pop bottle cut and taped into a homemade bong, rolling papers and piles of weed placed along the table. No pills, no coke and no ice.

Adrenaline pumped through my system and I fought the urge to throw him to the ground and beat a confession out of him. I needed to play this smart.

I leaned against the back of the sofa and trailed a fingertip along his shoulder teasingly. "Is that all you have to offer a girl? Some pot?"

He shared an excited look with his buddies, who were passing a pipe back and forth, but hadn't said a word yet. His look seemed to say "I told ya so" and I knew he'd told them that I was hot for him. Tim shifted on the shabby cushions and got closer to me, running his hand up a bit higher on my thigh. It was good thing I'd worn jeans or I might not've been able to stop myself from breaking a couple of his fingers.

"I've got a lot more than that to give you, but I thought I'd be a good host first."

Letting my tongue dart out and run across my bottom lip, I gave him a steamy look and whispered, "Why don't you grab some of that," I nodded at the table, "and you and I go have a little private party?"

"Oh yeah," he said in an excited drawl. He gave my thigh a squeeze before reaching for the altered pop bottle and other goodies. The idiot was so high and stupid he actually believed I was there to fuck him. He laughed at his buddies and boasted as he stood up. "See you losers later. Lex and I are gonna go have a good time."

I headed down the hallway to the back door and reached for the handle.

"Where are you going?"

Opening the door I tossed a suggestive wink over my shoulder. "I'm an adventurous girl. I find being outdoors is a big turn on."

He followed me out, giggling like a schoolgirl. We went down the three steps and went over to a picnic table that was near the side of the house. I stepped up on the seat and sat on the tabletop. Tim put the junk next to me and tried to step between my legs. I grabbed his roving hands and held them tight. Looking him in the eye I gave a small smile. "How about a joint first."

"Oh! Sure." He quickly moved to sit at the table next to me, his back against the tabletop and his shoulder against my leg. He pulled out a paper and started to expertly level out the marijuana across it.

"Who do you guys get your stuff from?" I deliberately made my voice soft and seductive as he worked. Acting like the party girl he thought I was.

"Bill, my buddy in there. His sister picks for a grow operation in B.C., and he gets some good shit from her when she visits."

"Really?" I fought to keep my tone casual, easygoing. "You don't have any local connections?"

"Well, yeah. But this stuff is way good. Better than what you'd get locally."

"I can't believe how hard it is to find a dealer. I've been trying ever since I started work at The Crib."

"That's cuz you work for Jimmy, and Jimmy hates dealers." He talked as he rolled, his voice lazy and relaxed. Stoned. "You need someone to hook you up before they trust you."

"But it's a biker bar. I figured I'd be able to find a hookup somehow. I mean, I heard a rumor that Jimmy was a dealer, and that he killed a guy a while ago for not paying him."

Tim shook his head slowly and started to roll the product between his fingers. "Nah. That wasn't Jimmy. Everyone who knows him knows he don't tolerate drugs or dealers, but he has a soft spot for users. Thinks he can save them or something."

"From smoking pot?" I gave a harsh laugh. "What's the big deal with pot?"

"A dealer's a dealer to him, but that guy that was killed was a crackhead. It's the hard shit he really cares about."

"Do you know where I can get some of that?" With a tug on the hair at the back of his head I tilted his face so our eyes met. I let my excitement show and made him think it was for the high. "Do you have a local connection for that? I'd love to get some crystal meth. Ice would be perfect."

"That's heavy shit, girl. Bill's just into this for himself, and a few friends."

Tilting my head I thrust out my chest and moved my hand to play with the hair curling over his ear teasingly. "That's too bad. I have a couple days off coming up, and when I smoke a little ice, I just want to fuck for days."

Tim stopped what he was doing and stared at me, dumbfounded by my stark words. I leaned close and breathed into his ear softly before speaking. "Hook me up, will you?"

His cheeks flushed and his eyes glowed bright in the dark yard as his hands stilled. "Maybe."

My gut clenched and my heart pumped adrenaline through my body. *He knows! He knows where to get it!* My instincts had been right on. Unable to sit still I jumped off the picnic table and stood in front of him.

"Do you get it from the hospital? That's got to be a good supply of quality ingredients!" I rocked on my heels, tweaking my excitement so it looked like I wanted the high, and not just information. "Do you have a stash?"

"Shit, no!" he cried, stopping what he was doing. "I don't get anything from the hospital but a paycheck. It's a good job too, I wouldn't want to fuck it up."

"Oh," I let my disappointment be heard. "Well, you said you could get it, can you get it now?"

"I said *maybe*." He shifted on the bench, licked the rolly to make it stick and twisted the ends. He was trying so hard to think I could almost see the smoke coming from his ears. Thinking was bad.

Stepping forward I straddled his knees, much the way I had Devon's short hours ago. Pushing the flash of memory aside, I concentrated on the job. This step was too important to screw up.

"Now would be really good." I took the joint from his hand and with a flick of his lighter got it going, letting tendrils of fragrant smoke ease from my parted lips. Tim's eyes were glued to my mouth, his hands gripping my hips, trying to pull me closer.

"Call your guy now," I urged, handing him the joint and trailing my hands across his cotton-covered chest.

He took a big pull on the joint, not saying anything, just

considering. I shifted forward on his lap, wiggling my butt onto his groin. "Please?"

"All right," he muttered, passing me the joint again, and cupping my ass. "I'll call him and see if he's got anything for us."

Placing the joint between my lips I pulled my cell phone from my pocket, giving him an extra wiggle. "I'm so excited. Here, sexy, set it up now so we can party for a few days."

He still hesitated so I rolled my hips and gave a tiny moan, and he reached for the phone eagerly. Sucking on the joint I pretended to inhale, and just pushed the smoke back out through my nostrils. A clear head was not something I was willing to give up.

"Wayne? Hey man, it's Tim." My heart stopped for a beat, then skipped ahead at warp speed. *Wayne? Did he say Wayne?*

My head swam as Tim continued to mutter into the phone, not noticing my sudden stillness. "Yeah, I know it's late, but I got a hot chick on my lap wanting some ice—you got any? Yeah? Okay, I'll drop by the bar after work tomorrow and pick it up."

He flipped the phone closed and tucked it back into my pocket before putting his hands on my waist and starting to run them over my body.

My throat was tight with fury, making my voice a whisper. "Wayne the cook?" The same guy that had been working for Jimmy since I was ten? The one that had been there when Mike died, and knew exactly how we all felt about drugs?

"Yeah." He chuckled, his hands going around to my back, trying to pull me closer. "Bet you didn't even suspect your best connection was so close to you, eh?"

Rage flowed through my veins, making it hard to breathe. I untangled myself from Tim and climbed off his lap in one smooth move. Without a word I turned and started toward the front of the house, pulling my phone from my pocket.

"Hey! Where you going? I thought we were going to party?" he cried out. "Whatever. He won't be at the bar now, it's closed."

I didn't turn around or acknowledge him in any way.

"Crazy bitch!"

That about summed up my mood.

11

Anger fought with confusion until I felt like I was going to explode. I strode from the backyard, the two emotions battling inside me as I fondled my phone.

Wayne? I thought. Wayne was the guy who was dealing out of the bar? The same guy who probably murdered the addict in the alley and is letting Jimmy take the fall? How could he do that? Jimmy gave him a job when he dropped out of high school. He had practically adopted him into the family as Mike's older brother!

I hit a mental brick wall and stopped dead in my tracks. Mike.

Mike had overdosed, and we'd never found out where he got the drugs. No one was with him when I found him, and nobody came forward when I asked who'd been partying with him. Could it have been Wayne then too?

The ugly truth began to sink in and I eyed the phone in my hand. Part of me wanted to rush back to the motel, wake up Devon and tell him everything I'd learned. For the first time in

246 / Sasha White

as long as I could remember, I wanted to trust someone. And that someone was a cop.

Uh-uh. I'd been doing things my own way for too long. I'd come to town to do a job, and I was going to do it. After I got *proper* evidence, I'd call Devon.

I pressed a few buttons and lifted the phone to my ear.

"I hope that's me you're calling."

I froze, and then turned slowly to find Devon leaning against the front of the house, arms settled across his chest. An eerie calm settled over me and my anger took on a cold focus.

"No, actually it wasn't." Flipping the phone closed I gave him a blank stare. "What are you doing here, Devon?"

"I followed you." He pushed off from the wall and walked toward me. "Over here."

I followed him around the privacy hedge and saw his bike parked another house down. No wonder I hadn't heard him drive up.

"What did you learn?" he asked as we strode down the sidewalk.

"Why do you care?" I debated with how much to tell him. How much to trust him.

"I care what happens to you."

I snorted, ignoring the tightness in my chest. "Yeah, right. Let's not kid ourselves, you were just getting a piece of ass while you worked a case."

He stopped abruptly and reached for me. I shook him off and shot him a look full of fury.

"Alexis—"

"That's a bad habit you have, you know? Calling me by my given name when I never actually told you what it was." I shoved my hands deep in my jacket pockets to keep from using them. I wasn't sure if I wanted to grab him and kiss him, or smack him, but neither was acceptable at this point. I had other things to deal with. "Right now you have two choices, Devon.

You can either help me do things my way, or walk away. What's it going to be?"

Planting his hands on his hips his stormy eyes met mine, and his lips tightened. He shook his head slowly, watching me carefully.

"I'm not a cop, Lexy. I'm here to help you. Tony and Jimmy hired me to watch over you while you poked around." He let out a heavy sigh. "I'm a private security specialist. . . . A bodyguard."

My heart lodged in my throat and I fought for breath. "A bodyguard?" Tony and Jimmy hired a *bodyguard* for me?

The realization hit me hard. They really didn't have any faith in me, did they? The macho men, despite the fact that I'd grown up, been on my own for more than ten years, and worked as a professional investigator . . . They still didn't have any faith in me.

But they'd obviously had some faith in him since they told him I figured him for a cop. Pain knifed through my chest, and I struggled to breathe. Devon reached for me again, but I shrugged him off, turning my back on him and taking a couple of steps away.

After a slow, steady count to ten, I turned back to him. *Fuck 'em.* Tony and Jimmy might not believe I could do the job, but I knew I could. I was already one step ahead of everyone. I knew who the guy dealing out of The Crib was.

"Well, since you're not a cop, I guess you're stuck helping me do things my way. Let's get out of here."

His gaze searched my face, and I could tell he wanted to say something more. But perceptive guy that he was, he knew it wasn't the smart thing to do. "Where are we going?"

Shifting through my mental Rolodex I rattled off an address. Wayne's address. Adrenaline coursed through my veins and my skin began to tighten, making my whole body sensitive to my surroundings. Devon climbed on the bike and handed me the helmet. I perched behind him, cradling him between my legs, and focused on nothing but the task in front of me.

"You can't just go in there and beat a confession out of him." Exasperation was clear in Devon's voice as he shook his head at me.

"And why not?"

We were stopped at a gas station not far from Wayne's. Devon had pulled in and cut the engine. Refusing to go any farther until I told him my plan. He'd shown no surprise when I told him it was Wayne I was after, but he wasn't keen on my seat of the pants approach to dealing with him.

"Because then it's just your word against his. You need solid proof."

"I've got enough proof. The bastard was going to let Jimmy rot in jail. He deserves whatever he gets."

"Lexy, what good is getting him to confess to you? You know damn well that your word against his won't put him behind bars. Stop. Think. Be smart about this."

"Yeah? And what's your smart idea? Call the cops? You know they'll never get a confession out of him and he'll walk."

"I have an idea, but you'll have to trust me."

Trust. Not my strong suit. Could I really trust a guy I just met with something this important? Shit, could I trust anyone?

The street was dark, and quiet in the way that it always is in the wee hours of the morning. Soon, day workers would be creeping out of beds, turning coffee makers and lights on, but right now, the night was peaceful.

Knowing that Wayne worked nights for the past fifteen years, I was confident he'd still be awake. A dim light in the living room and the muffled echoes of what sounded like the music channel on the television confirmed that for me. After pushing out a big lungful of air and giving myself an all-over body shake, I lifted a hand and rapped on the door.

There was movement and shuffling sounds inside the house, and footsteps coming toward me. I stared into the peephole. "Let me in, Wayne. I need to talk to you about Jimmy."

The rattling of chains, the click of a deadbolt, and the door swung open.

"Lexy, you okay?"

His expression was almost caring. There was worry in his eyes, and a tightness around his mouth. My fingers curled into my palms and I clenched my fists, barely suppressing the urge to wipe that fake expression off his face.

"Can I talk to you?" I asked.

"Of course, of course." He stepped back and waved me in. "What's going on?"

The screen door slammed shut behind me as I followed him into the living room. When he turned to face me I couldn't contain myself and my fist connected with his nose.

There was a sickening crunch and blood spurted out.

"What the fuck!?" He fell back against the entrance wall and grabbed his nose.

I sprang forward, slamming him against the wall when he tried to straighten up, and pinning him there with a forearm across his windpipe. I kicked his feet out wide and shoved a leg between his so he couldn't kick me.

"You're the dealer." I said it starkly. Firmly. There was no questioning in my tone, or forgiveness in my heart. I pulled the knife from my waistband, flipped it open and pressed the sharp tip between a couple of ribs. "You've been selling shit out of the bar, and you were going to let Jimmy go down for murder. Tell me why I shouldn't just kill you now."

Fear flashed in his eyes for a second, but it was replaced by anger real fast.

"I was just doing what I had to do! You think I can live comfortably on what I make as a cook? Or retire?" He gave a derisive laugh.

"What you *had* to do?" Rage flowed up inside me, my hands shook with the effort of not shoving the knife in deep. "You had to kill the addict in the alley, and you had to let the cops believe it was Jimmy?"

"It's not my fault they suspected Jimmy for that. I had nothing to do with it." He gasped, his hands pulling at my arm as I leaned into him, cutting off more of his air supply.

"Not your fault?" I lifted my leg and put some added pressure on his nuts. "When have you not had enough to get by? Jimmy treats you more than fair. You're like family, and you repay him by killing a guy, and letting him take the fall? How is it not your fault?"

Wayne's eyes had started to bulge and his struggles were weaker. He couldn't talk so I eased up on his throat a bit.

"Tell me why it's not your fault," I whispered. I gave him a little head butt, and he cried out sharply. Putting my face close to his, so my hurt and rage were clear for him to see, I gave him another chance to talk. "Tell me what happened."

"That crackhead Adam wouldn't leave me alone." His voice was hoarse, and trembled a little when he spoke. I wasn't sure if it was from anger or fear, and I didn't care. "I told him to go get help. That I wouldn't sell to him no more, but he wouldn't leave me alone. He came to the bar. He said he was going to tell Jimmy what I was doing and I couldn't let him do that. Jimmy would've killed me."

"So you killed him?"

"It was either me or him. I have no one to look after me but me, so I did what I had to do."

"Jimmy would've looked after you, you're family!"

"No. I'm not." He shook his head again, defeated, his eyes giving me a glimpse of bitterness. "I'm an employee. Jimmy does what he can for his staff, but we're still staff. I'm still staff."

"He treated you like a son." I stepped back, pocketing my knife and giving him room to breathe. And myself some distance for the next question. I couldn't trust myself with the knife for this. He was quiet, silent tears rolling down his cheeks as he slumped against the wall.

"Even before Mike overdosed."

The quiet words echoed in the hallway. Wayne raised his head and stared at me. This time there was no resentment, only regret . . . and fear.

"Did you have anything to do with Mike's death? Tell me, now!" My insides trembled, and my heart pounded, blood roaring in my ears.

"I was with him," he whispered.

"Did you sell him the drugs?"

"No! I was just getting high myself, and Mike said he wanted to try it. He had some sort of reaction to it and started convulsing, so I ran."

"And just left him there to die?"

When he nodded miserably, I saw red. "You bastard!"

My right leg snapped out and kicked him in the groin, dropping him to the ground. I stepped in, fists swinging. "You fucking little bastard! You killed him!"

Bands of steel wrapped around my waist and pulled me off him. Tears of rage and pain streamed down my cheeks as I screamed curses at Wayne, and stretched to get a few more kicks in. Devon lifted me off my feet, and pinned me up against the far wall. His muscled body sheltered me as he bent his head and crooned into my ear. "Shh, it's okay. You did good, babe. We got it all on tape, he's done."

I stopped fighting and gave into the tears, turning in his arms to curl into his chest. The scent of leather and Devon eased into my system, calming me. I could hear others moving around us; someone was reading Wayne his rights, others were searching the house.

He'd come through for me. He told me if I trusted him I'd get my chance at Wayne, and we'd get proper evidence. Judging by the men in uniform moving around us, he hadn't let me down.

12

———————

"You don't have to go back, you know."

"I know." I rolled up my last skirt and pushed it into my backpack before lifting my head and facing the two men in my hotel room. "But I'm not ready to stay here either."

Two days had passed since Wayne's arrest and this was the first time I'd seen Jimmy and Tony since then. They'd tried to see me before, but Devon had put them off for me while I dealt with the police, and the emotional fallout of that night. But now I was leaving, going back to Vancouver.

"I'm still mad at you guys for hiring Devon without telling me. And letting me think he was cop, when you knew he wasn't."

"We were worried about you. We know you're tough and strong, and smart. But you're still our little girl." Tony's hands gestured in the air, one hand reaching out to me, the other against his heart. His chocolate-brown eyes full of love.

A heavy sigh eased its way through my throat. "I know that. It just really hurts that you two didn't have faith that I would find the guy."

None of us had talked about the fact that it had been Wayne.

The big strong Italian men wouldn't share their feelings of betrayal with me, and I'd shared all of mine with Devon. That had been enough.

"That's just it, baby girl. We knew you would find out who it was, and we were worried you'd go after him yourself. It was a killer you were looking for and we didn't want to have to go to your funeral any time soon." Jimmy stepped closer and pulled me into a bear hug. "Plus, we know your temper. We figured if Devon wasn't needed to save you, then he'd be needed to keep you from killing the dealer and going to jail yourself."

A weight lifted from my chest, and I knew he was right. If Devon hadn't been there, I could very well have been in jail myself.

"Okay, okay. I forgive you." I let go of Jimmy and opened my arms to my Uncle Tony. "Now come here and say goodbye properly."

Peace seeped over me as Tony wrapped his arms around me and clutched me to him, whispering in my ear. "I love you."

"I love you, too."

The rumbling purr of a powerful motorcycle signaled Devon's arrival and I pulled back. Picking up my backpack I slung it over my shoulder and reached for the door handle. We all trooped outside to stand by Devon's bike and have a last round of hugs. I climbed behind Devon and gazed at the two fathers in my life while securing my helmet.

"Don't look so sad, boys. I may be going back to Vancouver for now, but Edmonton is home. I'll be back."

I wrapped my arms tight around Devon's waist and nodded to him to leave. Jimmy and Tony waved as we pulled away and I blew them a kiss. "I love you guys!"

Devon aimed the bike south and we headed to the airport. The late summer wind was cool, even through my jeans, so I snuggled up tight against the warm body in front of me to enjoy the ride.

As good as it felt to know that Jimmy was safe, it hurt to know that Wayne had been the bad guy from the start. Someone we'd all thought was a friend, part of the family, had deceived us for years. He'd confessed to the police as soon as he'd been released from the hospital. I'd given him a broken nose, a fractured cheekbone and a slight concussion, but he'd refused to press charges.

Smart move.

My heart ached when I thought about how Mike died, how he'd thought he was with a friend, and how maybe, just maybe, he'd have lived if Wayne had called 911 instead of running away. But then I'd think of how Devon had called a friend of his, a detective who had agreed to let me go in and get the confession from Wayne, and my heart swelled.

Devon had stayed next to me during it all. He was there when the police questioned me, when they took my statement. When I went back to the motel and cried myself to sleep, he'd just held me close and made me feel safe. He gave me hope that good things could happen to good people.

It wasn't love. I wasn't even sure I could ever love romantically. But, he'd earned my trust and my friendship, and that went a long way.

The bike slowed as we approached the airport, and I waved him past the parking lot and toward the main doors. I didn't want him to come inside with me. I hated long good-byes. He pulled up to the curb in front of the departure gates and shut off the Spirit.

I jumped off the back and fumbled with the safety strap under my chin. He swung a leg over the bike but remained seated. Hooking his fingers in my belt loops he pulled me between his spread thighs. "Come 'ere."

I scanned his dark features as he worked the closure and re-moved my helmet before settling his hands on my hips. His eyes lifted to mine and I remembered when he'd walked away from me in the storeroom that first night. It seemed longer than five days ago.

"Two of a kind, huh?" I whispered.

He lips spread into a full-blown smile, flashing white teeth. "You betcha, darlin'."

I leaned forward and touched his lips with mine. A slow swipe of my tongue and I was inside, getting a last taste of heaven. I pulled back slowly, sucking in deep breaths.

"I'll be seeing you again," I whispered as I stepped away, starting for the terminal.

Devon crossed his arms over his chest and flashed me the cocky grin that made my heart pound and my pussy drool. "Yes, you will."

Walk on the wild side with WOLF TALES II, a sizzling new paranormal from Kate Douglas. Available now from Aphrodisia . . .

The hand cupping Tia's breast was warm and rough, both palm and fingertips callused. Her nipple rose to a painful, unbelievably sensitive peak, pinched between a blunt thumb and forefinger. Her vagina actually pulsed with each beat of her heart as a moist tongue followed a line from her breastbone to her navel, then dipped inside and swirled. She shivered, caught in that sensual state between sleep and wakefulness, her arousal growing with each gentle caress.

Lapping slowly, surely, the long, slick and very mobile tongue now swept the crease of her buttocks then delved between her sensitive labia and licked deeply into her pussy. She caught back a cry as the fiery trail swept upwards, barely teasing at her clit before sliding once more across her lower belly.

Spreading her legs even wider, slipping lower in her seat, she raised one eyelid to get a better view of her lover.

Time stood still—painfully, irrevocably, still.

A wolf stared back at her, amber eyes glowing, tongue still lapping slowly at her belly, his ivory canines curved like sharpened sabers. He looked up and slowly licked his muzzle, wrapping that long, rough tongue almost all the way around.

The scream caught in her throat.

A soothing voice clicked into Tia's consciousness and shattered the image crouched between her knees.

"We've started our descent into San Francisco International airport and are currently flying at 27,500 feet. If you're on the left side of the plane you should be able to look out your window and see Half Dome in Yosemite, sticking up like a . . ."

Tia gasped. Her lungs pumped like a bellows and her skin flushed from hot to cold. She blinked rapidly, noted the older man next to her still snored, blissfully asleep. Scooting quickly back in her seat, Tia sat upright and smoothed her wrinkled denim skirt. Her breath escaped in a long sigh. For extra measure, she fastened her seatbelt, pulled it firmly across her middle and prayed the moisture between her legs hadn't soaked through the denim.

Damn the dreams. Until last week, she hadn't had any this explicit in almost three months. Why now? Tia glanced once more at the man sleeping next to her and flushed, her skin once again going hot and cold all over. What if he'd awakened? What if someone had seen her, sprawled out, legs spread wide, lips parted and breasts heaving?

She cupped her forehead in the palm of her hand and shuddered. Damn, this had better be the right choice, this move back to San Francisco. Somehow she needed to understand the dreams, the explicit, sensual dreams that had finally broken the link between her and Shannon, Tia's dearest friend in the world.

Her friend and her lover. She'd been with Shannon for ten years, ever since they were teenagers heading off to boarding school together, their hormones in high gear and their need for one another overwhelming. It had been so good then, so perfect, both emotionally and physically.

Tia sighed. She missed the intensity of their teenaged affair, the forbidden nature of love with another female, the heart-stopping, lung-bursting climaxes they'd managed to wring out of one another. So good at first. So fulfilling, for a time, at least, then slowly, surely, Tia had acknowledged something important was missing.

So had Shannon. The last five years their relationship had merely been a safety net for both of them. A safety net held together by friendship and only rarely, sexual love.

Even Shannon admitted to occasional sex with a man, something Tia enjoyed as well, but it had never been enough. Not with one man, not even with multiple partners. The sense of something else, something more powerful, more sensual, lured her out of every relationship, away from any commitment.

Away from Shannon.

The dreams hadn't helped. Explicit, arousing, forbidden dreams. Always the wolf, amber eyes glowing, teeth sharp and glistening, the rough, mobile tongue lapping, licking . . . Tia blinked away the image and scrubbed at her wrists and forearms. Why, when she remembered the dreams, did her skin crawl? She hated it, the itchy, agitating sense of something just beneath the surface. Sometimes she wondered if she were losing her mind, descending into some unexplainable madness.

The plane jerked a bit as it descended. The FASTEN SEAT BELT sign blinked overhead. An attendant leaned close, awakened the man sleeping next to Tia and asked him to fasten his belt. She smiled at Tia and moved on to the next sleeping passenger.

Tia shook off the strange sensations and her thoughts returned to Shannon. If her father had only known how close the girls were when they'd asked to go away to boarding school together, he might have forbidden it. Obviously, he didn't have a clue. In fact, the poor man had been so relieved when Tia left it was almost embarrassing.

It couldn't have been easy for him, raising a daughter without her mother there for guidance. Coping with hormones and emotions completely foreign to him, not to mention the issues that occasionally arose because of her biracial status. Maybe Tia and Shannon wouldn't have become lovers if they'd had mothers, but Shannon's mom had died of cancer when Shannon was only five. That shared loss had drawn the girls together.

Tia's mother had been murdered. To this day she didn't know all the details, only that her father had never even talked of remarrying. He'd loved her mother beyond all women.

He'd loved Tia as if she were a princess, put her on a pedestal. *More like a perch,* she thought, *locked securely in a gilded cage.* Rationally, she knew he'd wanted to protect her, but he'd merely driven Tia away.

What would it be like now, to live in the same city, to see her father whenever she wanted, to finally learn more about his life? She'd have a chance, maybe, to learn the details of her mother's murder. More important, she'd have the freedom her adult status now gave her to search for answers.

Tia sighed. She wished she remembered her mother more clearly, but the image she carried of Camille's smile was the face in the snapshots, the pictures both Tia and her father treasured.

Ulrich had always had presence, as far as Tia was concerned. She wondered how he did now that he was partially retired. From his letters and calls and their infrequent visits, Tia knew he was still active and involved, busy with his detective agency. He'd always had a lot of friends.

Lucien Stone's image popped into Tia's mind. *Luc.* She hadn't seen him since the summer before she and Shannon went off to Briarwood, but he and her father had always been close. He was probably married by now with a couple of kids, but he'd filled her fantasies for years. When Shannon made love to her, it was Luc's mouth tasting, licking, driving her over the edge. When Shannon had used a vibrator or dildo between Tia's legs, Tia had been filled by Luc.

She stared out the window, watching the multi-colored squares in San Francisco Bay as they glided down over the salt beds, and tried to picture Lucien Stone with ten years added to his stern yet boyish good looks.

By the time the plane landed and Tia unbuckled her seat belt, she had an image in her mind of a pot-bellied, middle-aged man with thinning hair.

When she reached for her carry-on luggage in the overhead rack, Tia added bad teeth and an earring. She was grinning as she walked down the enclosed ramp to the gate, the image of an older Lucien Stone taking on cartoon properties in her over-active imagination.

She was still smiling when she arrived at the luggage carousal. Her father waited there, just as overwhelming and handsome as when she'd last seen him, his skin ruddy from wind and sun, his hair a thick shock of white badly in need of a trim. Ulrich pulled her into a hug, his big arms and broad chest erasing every misgiving Tia had felt about coming home.

He smelled just the same as always, a combination of Dial soap and Colgate shaving cream. Tia took deep breaths, just to absorb his beloved scent.

"Sweetie, you are absolutely gorgeous."

Her father stood back for a better look, his big hands clasped tightly to her shoulders. "I've missed you. I'm glad you're home."

Tia's eyes filled with tears. She wanted nothing more than to throw herself back into her father's arms and tell him how lonely she'd been, how much she'd wanted to come home.

How terribly glad she was to be back. "It's good to be here, Daddy."

"Was the trip okay?" He reached for the bag she grabbed off the carousal, set it on the floor and then snatched another she pointed to.

"Yeah. Just long. I . . ." No. It couldn't be. Not Luc? A chill raced along her spine, a sense of awareness that left her weak-kneed and shivering.

"Hello, Tia."

"Luc? Good Lord! I haven't seen you since . . ."

"Since you were a skinny little sixteen-year-old with braces on your teeth." Smiling, Luc stepped forward and drew her into a friendly, brotherly hug.

At least Tia assumed it was meant to be brotherly. Where her father's hug had been home and comfort, Luc's was bed and beyond. His big hands stroked her spine, the briefest of contacts that left her feeling naked an wanted. His lips brushed her cheek and she fought the urge to lean closer for more. She breathed deeply of his scent. He was spice and fresh air, deep woods and dark rivers . . . intoxicating and addictive.

When he released her—was it only seconds later?—Tia clamped her jaws together to keep her teeth from chattering. "Luc, you look . . . you haven't . . ." Her voice drifted off and she realized she was staring at him.

He grinned, obviously aware of her discomfort. His teeth were perfectly straight and very white. His nose wasn't nearly as straight, but the bump on the bridge where he'd probably broken it at some time during the past ten years only made him look stronger, more masculine.

Tia blinked. The dream she'd had earlier on the plane materialized in all its sensual detail. Damn, Lucien Stone looked exactly like that hungry wolf with his deep-set amber eyes and feral grin. It was much too easy to picture him kneeling between her thighs, his tongue lapping away at her cream.

Tia gulped, no ladylike swallow at all, but Luc ignored her faux pas and instead reached past her to pick up the last two of her large bags off the carousal. He slung one over his shoulder and gripped the other easily in his left hand, then grabbed the two smaller ones in his right. Ulrich took Tia's carry-on bag from her and led the way to the parking garage.

Tia followed quietly, her inner thighs sliding moistly, one against the other, with each step. The two men were discussing something, but the words merely sailed past her without sense. Awareness of Luc screamed a steady beat inside her brain, echoed in the rhythmic clenching between her legs. Her chest felt tight and her skin itchy and she'd never been this aware of another human being in her life.

Tia didn't think to question how Luc had identified her mismatched set of bags out of all the others on the luggage carousel until he shoved them into the trunk and shut the lid.

Somehow, he'd found them without her help. But how? Tia turned to ask but Luc opened the door and gestured with his hand. She smiled as he seated her in the front. Ulrich stepped back on the curb when Luc moved around to the driver's side and climbed into the Mercedes.

Frowning, Tia lowered the window. "Dad? Aren't you coming with us?"

Ulrich smiled, leaned close and kissed Tia's cheek. "I've got a meeting in Burlingame so I'll catch a cab. Luc will get you settled, then I want him to bring you out for dinner this evening. Is that okay with you?"

Tia nodded, blinking nervously. Like she had a choice? Why did this feel planned, as if the two men followed a script? She glanced once more at her father and realized he was looking steadily at Luc. If she didn't know better, Tia would have thought Ulrich and Luc communicated without speaking. She turned to Luc, noticed his slight nod, and when she looked back at her father it was to see his broad shoulders and back as he walked purposefully out of the parking garage without another word.